She couldn't take her eyes off this hero

That sexy, muscular, masculine body who'd come to her rescue. When Cody bent to reach for his jeans, she said just one word.

"Please..."

The word sounded loud in the quiet of the motel room. He looked at her, disbelieving. Puzzled. But also desiring her. He couldn't hide it any more than she could.

Jen held out her hand. She was acting on pure instinct, wanting to reaffirm life in the most primal way possible. Her throat felt dry, constricted with both fear and excitement.

He moved toward her on the bed, his eyes wide, his growing arousal evident.

She wanted to take him into her arms and offer him peace. It would be pleasant. No... Pleasant couldn't begin to describe her sexual feelings toward Cody.

I want you, she thought, *as I've never wanted another man in my life.* With a single touch she knew she would set something in motion. Something that was always meant to be. Destiny. Kismet.

This was more than just sex.

Dear Reader,

When I looked up the word *hero* in my dictionary, there were several meanings, among them a mythological or legendary figure of great strength and authority. A man admired for his achievements and qualities, or a chief male in literary and dramatic work. Or perhaps a hero is a person who does brave deeds, like the main character in a movie.

There are many definitions, but we all know a hero when we see one. Someone rises to the occasion and becomes the best person he or she can be. The New York City firemen who displayed extraordinary courage in the face of absolute disaster that day in September. A best friend who keeps others going through tough times and despair. Or someone who hopes, and acts, against impossible odds.

Cody Roberts, the hero in *Rescue Me!,* is such a person. Faced with deadly odds, he chose to act. And in so doing, he changed the lives of three people, himself included, forever. I loved writing his AMERICAN HEROES story, and I hope you will all enjoy reading it, as well.

All my best,

Elda Minger

ELDA MINGER
RESCUE ME!

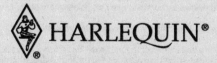

HARLEQUIN®

TORONTO • NEW YORK • LONDON
AMSTERDAM • PARIS • SYDNEY • HAMBURG
STOCKHOLM • ATHENS • TOKYO • MILAN • MADRID
PRAGUE • WARSAW • BUDAPEST • AUCKLAND

To Nancy Cochran.
You are a heroine in real life, and this story is for you.
I'm so lucky to have you as a friend.

ISBN 0-373-69223-4

RESCUE ME!

Copyright © 2005 by Elda Minger.

This edition published by arrangement with Harlequin Books S.A.

® and TM are trademarks of the publisher. Trademarks indicated with
® are registered in the United States Patent and Trademark Office, the
Canadian Trade Marks Office and in other countries.

www.eHarlequin.com

Printed in U.S.A.

1

CODY ROBERTS HAD SUFFERED through worse hangovers, but he couldn't remember when.

His mouth tasted like the inside of a sewer. His eyes were gritty. He had to get to his job by noon, show up and convince everyone he could still do it. And he'd never felt less like going to work in his life.

But he had no choice. Especially not with his reputation. People he worked with depended on him. And more than that, he wanted to be able to depend on himself again.

Even though Cody wasn't drunk, he drove carefully along the Arizona road, watching out for other cars. He wasn't so hungover that he was a danger to others. No, if he'd been that wasted, he wouldn't have gotten behind the wheel of a car.

As low as he'd gotten various times in the last seven years, he'd never sink *that* low.

Fortified by a cup of black coffee from a convenience store a few miles back, Cody drained the last of the surprisingly good coffee and tossed the empty cup into the back of the rusty old blue van. With just a little more caffeine he'd be ready to head back to work.

Up ahead, just as the sun began to break over the

horizon, he saw the familiar logo of another chain convenience store. Though desert sunrises were spectacularly beautiful, painting the skies with lavenders, pinks and golds, Cody didn't allow himself the pleasure of enjoying nature's gifts. He had a cup of coffee to get and a job to finish up this October morning—in that order.

JENNIFER WHITNEY STARED AT the front of the convenience store, wondering if she had enough energy to walk inside.

She'd been driving most of the night. Now, just east of Phoenix, off Interstate 10, she had to decide if she was going to take a detour on her way to Los Angeles by way of Sedona. She wanted to see those red rocks and energy vortexes and the Indian ruins and had planned on making this detour when she'd first started out.

But now she was wiped out. Perhaps the wisest thing to do would be to forget the coffee, find the nearest motel, check in and sleep for a good twelve hours. She needed to rest. More than that, she needed the sanctuary of a motel room in order to forget her problems. And they were considerable.

The need for coffee won out. She stretched, then grimaced as she heard all the little cricks and pops of her protesting body when she moved. Determined to get some coffee and hit the road again, Jen stepped out of the car and went into the store.

CUTE BUTT.

That was Cody's first thought as he pulled into the

convenience store parking lot. He eased the van to a stop on the far side of the parking lot, needing the little bit of a walk to stretch his legs and get some air.

The petite blonde had caught his eye the minute she'd walked into the store. He observed her through the glass, enjoying the view as she headed straight for the coffee.

Cute butt, he thought again. *And a great car.* The candy-apple-red Mustang sat in the parking lot, directly in front of the convenience store, the backseat piled high with boxes, blankets and what looked like a small table. He imagined that the trunk was crammed just as tightly.

She was moving. On the road.

He thought about talking to her, then realized he probably looked like the devil himself. After a long, lost weekend, he had a certain griminess about him, and certainly from the way his eyes were stinging and sensitive, they had to be bloodshot.

Hardly the best first impression to make on a lady.

And she was a lady. He'd registered that fact right away. The way she carried herself, the way she wore her clothing, even though she was dressed in jeans and a light pink sweater. He'd seen the slender gold bracelet flash on her arm in the early morning autumn sun.

For just an instant Cody wondered what a woman like that was doing alone on the road. Didn't she have family to take care of her? A friend to drive with? The open road could be tough. Even dangerous. It wasn't wise for a woman to travel alone, and she looked about as substantial as a cream puff.

Aw, so he looked like hell. He could at least go in,

get that cup of coffee and wish that cutie a fine morning.

He smiled at that thought and reached for the door handle to the van. Cody was just about to step outside when a man, late twenties or very early thirties, dressed in ripped jeans, a black T-shirt and a jean jacket and boots, caught his eye. Long, stringy, dirty hair. Rounding the corner from behind the convenience store. He looked tired. Fed up.

And he was carrying a sawed-off shotgun.

JEN HAD JUST ADDED AN EXTRA packet of sugar to her coffee. Baby coffee, her friends in Chicago would have teased. She always liked to add a lot of milk, otherwise it tended to upset her stomach. She was sensitive to caffeine, so she knew that even with the small amount of coffee in the cup she'd get enough of a buzz to drive a little farther and find a room. Then finally she could crash.

She knew she must be really wiped because she was starting to have doubts about the wisdom of this entire trip. When she'd started out from Chicago, she'd been so confident that she was doing the right thing. But it got awfully lonely out on the road, and she'd had plenty of time since leaving home to question what she was doing.

She approached the counter, coffee in hand, eyeing the display of doughnuts nearby and wondering if she should go for broke and get one.

"Oh, go for it."

She glanced up and smiled at the young man behind the counter. He had sandy brown hair, clear blue eyes and his face was sprinkled with freckles. Those eyes were amused as he gazed at her. He wore a faded gray sweatshirt and equally worn jeans.

She recognized a fellow optimist when she saw one. Still, he did seem awfully young to be in charge of the store.

"You're the only one here?"

He seemed affronted, but in a kidding way. "Hey, Charlie couldn't make it, so he asked me to cover for him."

Well, that explained it. Jen couldn't help smiling back at him. "How much are the dough—"

The front door exploded inward, and a man with long, greasy black hair yelled, "Get down, both of you! On the floor!"

And the nightmare began.

CODY HAD WATCHED AS THE MAN entered the convenience store. If there had ever been a sign from God for him to stop drinking, this was it. More than anything he wished he had a clearer head.

A girl with a gold bracelet and a kid behind a counter who looked as if he was barely out of high school—two people as good as dead unless he got in there and did something. He didn't think scum like that would let either of them live, because then they'd be able to identify him.

Weighing his options, trying to come up with a plan to get everyone out alive, Cody stealthily moved across the parking lot.

"THE MONEY! HURRY UP!"

The cashier's voice was shaking so badly, he could barely get the words out. "I can't open the register, I can't just—"

For one awful moment Jen thought the man was going to shoot the boy right where he stood.

"Ring up a bogus sale, asshole, before I blow your head off!"

Jen lay facedown on the floor. She'd dropped her coffee, flung it in a reflex reaction, and it had spilled all over the floor several feet away. She tried to breathe, tried to think, to remain calm. But it was so hard. Her heart was thundering in her chest; she could hear her blood pounding sickeningly in her ears. For a long, still moment, the longest moment, almost out of time, she had the strongest intuition she and this boy were going to die.

Right here. Right now.

Life over. Finished.

"Whoa, wait a minute."

Everything within her stilled as the robber turned his attention toward her.

"Sit up and take off that bracelet. And keep those hands where I can see them."

She sat up as slowly as she dared, hoping perhaps the young clerk could press a silent alarm button or something while he wasn't being watched. But he didn't have a chance. This man had done this sort of thing before, his dark eyes feverish as his glance darted back and forth between them.

He was drunk or high or both. And that was bad for the two of them, making this man all the more unpredictable.

"Take it off!"

She did.

"Throw it here."

The oddest memory, considering her circumstances, surfaced. Her high school graduation and her father handing her the small, beautifully wrapped package. The happiness on his handsome face when she'd opened his present and he'd seen her joy.

She tossed the robber the bracelet carefully. She'd considered hurling it so he'd have trouble catching it, but she didn't want to do anything to make matters even worse. This was real life, not some action movie.

"Nice." The robber studied it briefly, then shoved it in his jean-jacket pocket. "Now the sweater."

She felt nauseous as his meaning became clear.

"Hurry it up!" He glanced toward the clerk. "Get that money out, asshole!" Then back at her. "The sweater, babe. *Now!*"

Looking down the barrel of a loaded shotgun didn't give her much of a choice or any sense of false modesty. Jen started to pull the pink cashmere sweater over her head. Slowly. Slowly. Thinking the entire time that she would rather die than have this man touch her.

CODY HAD TO MAKE SURE THIS guy was alone. That took a few minutes, but he hadn't heard any gunshots yet, so he still had hope.

While he'd sneaked out in back of the convenience store, he'd formulated a plan.

Help me out here, okay? he prayed silently. *At least let the two of them live. If this is the way you want my*

*sorry ass to go, I accept it. But those two in there, they
don't deserve it—*

Taking a deep breath, he kicked the front door open.

SHE'D JUST PULLED THE SWEATER over her head, still
had her hands entangled in its sleeves, when she
heard the noise.

Someone else—

"Hey, you!" the slurred, masculine voice said.
"Whadda I have ta do ta get a cuppa—" He stumbled
into the robber, causing him to turn.

Causing him to take the shotgun off her.

A drunk. Great.

Then the drunk moved so he was between her
and the robber, then he turned, pretending to sneeze.
His face angled so the robber couldn't get a look at
his expression, this crazy stranger gave her a look so
full of fierce command, she almost shrank back. He
inclined his head ever so slightly toward the counter,
the movement miniscule.

And Jen realized he was no drunk.

The unspoken command in his eyes was unmis-
takable.

Get behind that counter. Now.

She did, crabbing back on her hands and knees,
moving sideways over the slick linoleum floor, trying her best not to make any noise as the "drunk"
continued to talk.

"Okay, okay! Hands up, I get it!" The stranger
backed away from the robber, and Jen noticed he was
doing an excellent job of keeping the man's shotgun
pointed toward his midsection—away from her and

the young clerk. She couldn't believe what she was seeing.

"Goddamn it, I said *up!* Up in the air, you bastard."

What happened next went down so fast, she didn't see all of it. The stranger moved so quickly, butting headlong into the robber and blessedly avoiding the shotgun. The gun flew up and fired, and chunks of the ceiling rained down, clattering against the linoleum. Jen got behind that counter in no time, and the young clerk threw himself down on top of her, covering her, then putting his hands over his ears, his wiry young body shaking as hard as hers was.

Then the sounds of fists.

One punch. A grunt. Two punches.

Then silence.

The clerk was crying, and Jen smoothed his short hair back from his face, offering comfort. She used her cashmere sweater, still tangled around her arms, to wipe his eyes. And hoped to God that their stranger was the one still standing.

She had the sobbing boy cradled against her as she looked up. The stranger leaned over the counter and smiled, his split lip bleeding.

"Guess I can't ask him if he has any rope."

"By the—by the car stuff, the oil and stuff," the clerk gasped, then continued to cry. Jen's eyes stung as she held him closer.

"Great. Be right back after I tie our friend up."

She heard each decisive step as he strode across the store, paused, then walked back. Heard him unwinding rope. Then she almost started to cry herself as she pictured him tying up the man who had almost taken all of their lives.

"I'm okay," the clerk gasped. "I'm okay."

"Sure?"

"Yeah. Yeah. I've gotta call my boss."

"Call the police first."

The boy was in no shape to do anything. Gently disengaging herself, Jen stood up, reached for the phone behind the counter and dialed 911.

"Where are we?"

"Don't worry," the clerk said, then blew his nose. She recognized the signs of masculine embarrassment in his eyes. "The address will come up on their screen."

He glanced up as the stranger approached and placed a large cup of black coffee on the counter, then selected two raspberry doughnuts from the display and put them in a waxed paper bag.

He set the bag next to the coffee and smiled wearily at them. "Just tell 'em there's been a robbery and their man is right here, all hog-tied and waiting for them." He reached into his back jean pocket and took out his wallet.

"I really don't think—" Jen began.

He threw down a ten-dollar bill. "That should cover the rope, the coffee and the doughnuts. How's he doing?"

"Okay, but—"

He walked over to a display, plucked down a small, travel-sized packet of tissues, then leaned over the counter, making eye contact with the clerk on the floor.

"You did real good, son," he said, handing him the tissues. "You didn't lose your head."

The boy simply nodded.

The stranger picked up his coffee and bag of doughnuts, then started toward the door.

"But—" Jen said. "The police are coming. Aren't you going to stay and—"

He held up his hand. "I've got to go. People are depending on me."

"But—"

He smiled, then grimaced in mild pain as the expression pulled his split lip taut. "Darlin', I wish I could stay, but I can't. You'd better get dressed—the police should be here shortly."

Jen glanced down. Clad only in a delicate, lacy demibra, she might as well have been topless in front of him. But it didn't bother her. Not now. She'd almost been killed.

"Wait!" She pulled her sweater over her head, flipping her long hair out of the neckline. "Wait! I don't even know your name or how to thank you or—"

"You don't want to know me," he said and walked out the door.

2

REACTION SET IN AS CODY pulled out of the parking lot.

His hand—his right hand holding his coffee—started to shake. Setting the cup down in the van's drink holder, he concentrated on driving. If the van lurched along at a slightly slower pace than was normal for this stretch of road, that was all right. The sun wasn't very high in the sky and there wasn't much traffic.

Two black-and-white police cars whizzed by, lights flashing, sirens screaming, racing toward the convenience store. Cody watched their progression in his rearview mirror, then turned his attention back to the desert road.

He couldn't have stayed. The press would have had a field day. He could see the headline in the tabloids now: Washed Up Action Hero Makes a Real Rescue. Or worse. No, he wanted no part of it. He'd seen firsthand how the media destroyed people's lives.

Hell, he'd been one of their supreme achievements.

He drove until he reached a shopping center, complete with grocery store, drugstore, dry cleaner, pet shop, a bagel shop, a health-food store and a Mexican restaurant. Feeling as if he were operating the van in slow motion, he guided it into the parking lot, where he chose a parking space on the far side of the stores. Turning off the ignition, he sat in the driver's seat, staring ahead, seeing nothing.

Talk about a wake-up call. Today had been nothing short of a sharp smack to the side of his head.

He didn't know how long he sat there, but finally he shook his head and reached for the bag of jelly doughnuts. He ate first one, then the other, then drank some of the strong, warm coffee. Just the ordinary feel of eating something, just the everyday smell of coffee, the taste of powdered sugar and raspberry jelly, was enough for him right now.

It comforted him.

Cody closed his eyes, then opened them quickly as he saw brief flashes of the robbery in his mind. Better to see what was actually out there. He focused his gaze on a cactus on the side of the parking lot and took a few deep breaths.

He'd been scared to death going into that store. But all he'd known was that he couldn't let those two people inside die. Both of them so young and filled with promise. Both thinking they had all the time in the world when he knew that wasn't true at all.

Older and wearier—but not necessarily wiser—he knew better than to take an optimistic attitude to life.

He checked his watch. He didn't have to report to the set until noon, so he could afford to take a short nap. Even though he knew he probably wouldn't sleep, he needed to breathe, to feel, to close his eyes and center himself. He could still feel the adrenaline buzzing through his bloodstream.

Thankful that the van only possessed its two front seats, while the rest of the vehicle was used for hauling equipment around, Cody got out of his seat and maneuvered himself into the back of the van. Someone had left an old sleeping bag there, and he unzipped it and spread it out, knowing it would offer his back some cushioning against the metal floor of the van. He stretched out on top of the thick material.

And thought about the blond woman. He wondered how she was feeling, where she'd been going, what was going to happen to her now. He wondered what would have happened if there had been no robbery this morning and if he'd been able to talk to her while she'd made her purchases.

Something about her had pulled at him. A flare of attraction. But something else.

He sighed. Stretched. Closed his eyes. Tried not to replay the robbery in his mind. Thought of his father's ranch in Texas, the way it had been. The creek. Quarter horses grazing. The wind singing through the trees, the green tops and silvery undersides of the leaves making that subtle contrast in the sun. The smell of the earth. The feel of that sun on his shoulders.

It worked. Slowly but surely it worked. Despite the odds, he found a measure of peace.

JEN DIDN'T FEEL ANYTHING until she saw the young cashier's mother enter the convenience store. An attractive brunette in her late thirties, she strode right over to her son, enfolding him in her arms.

"Oh, Johnny, are you all right?" Jen heard as the concerned female voice floated out from behind the counter. And as she watched mother and son, her eyes filled.

Her own mother had died when she was seven. Cancer had taken her quickly. Her father had provided Jen with every material comfort, except for the things she had really craved—love, understanding, acceptance and his time. Now, in this convenience store, if her father had come to help her, the first words out of his aristocratic mouth would have been blame. He was a master at assigning blame and instilling guilt. Something along the lines of *What did you do?*

She wondered if the clerk—Johnny—knew how very lucky he was.

She answered all the questions put to her by the police officers as best as she could. Concerned for Johnny, Jen sensed he felt the robbery was somehow his fault, or at least he didn't believe he'd handled it as well as he could have. Needing to reassure him, perhaps as much for herself as for him, she approached the back of the store, where mother and son were now sitting.

Johnny had told the officers his full name was John McGann. Jen directed her attention to the young man's mother. She didn't think Johnny was in any shape to hear what she wanted to say.

"Mrs. McGann?" she said.

The clerk's mother glanced up, her skin pale, her hazel eyes worried.

"I just wanted you to know your son was very brave. When—when we were behind the counter and we couldn't see what was going on, he used his body to protect me. He would have—" She didn't have to go on. All three of them knew what would have happened.

"Who was this man?" Mrs. McGann whispered, obviously referring to the stranger who had subdued the robber. "Why didn't he stay?"

"I don't know. But—but I thanked him. I—"

I don't even know your name or how to thank you or—

Actually she hadn't. She'd tried to, but she hadn't.

"Well, he was an angel, protecting the two of you," the older woman said. She eyed Jen. "Are you all right, hon? Would you like to come back home with us and have a cup of coffee or something? Maybe talk about it a little?"

When Jen didn't answer, she said, "Do your folks live nearby? Is there anyone I can call to come and be with you?"

Another employee had arrived, ready to take over, as Johnny was clearly being given the rest of the day off. Jen hesitated. There had always been that part of her that had yearned for a mother, and Mrs. McGann was obviously a very good one, offering nurturing and support to her during the aftermath of this crisis. But Jen had a sudden intuition that if she didn't get back on the road immediately, she might lose her nerve altogether and hightail it back to Chicago and the life her father wanted for her.

"That's very kind, but I have to be in Phoenix later this morning." Which was a lie. She had no one waiting for her in Phoenix. No one at all.

"I understand," Mrs. McGann said, but Jen had the feeling she saw much more than she commented on. Funny how most mothers had that funny little sixth sense that clued them in to what was really going on. "But if you need to talk or anything, here's my number. I'll give you both home and work. And my cell. You can call me anytime. Anytime at all." She scribbled the phone numbers on a piece of paper and handed it to her.

"Thank you, Mrs. McGann."

"Laura. Call me Laura. And thank you for staying with Johnny until the police arrived. Until I arrived."

"Of course."

After making sure the police didn't want her to remain for any more questioning and taking their card and giving them her cell number, Jen poured herself a large cup of coffee. She laced it with plenty of milk and sugar, took two of the glazed doughnuts, paid for her purchases over Johnny's protests and walked outside to her Mustang.

The sage-scented desert air stung her nostrils as she breathed in deeply, and for one long moment she thought she was going to cry. There had been that moment, inside the store and on the floor, when she'd thought she'd never take another breath, and it felt so wonderful to still be alive. The sky, the air, the coffee—everything felt unbearably new, almost shimmering with life.

I'll never take it for granted again.

Though little more than an hour had passed since she'd first entered the convenience store, Jen felt as if she were entering another lifetime. Though she was profoundly grateful to be alive, something crucial had been lost.

She'd realized how easy and inconsequential it was for some people to take a life, and that dark knowledge made her exhausted to her bones, to the depths of her soul.

And afraid.

As she unlocked her car, she thought of the man who had come to their rescue. He'd been tall and strong, and those blue eyes had been so intense when he'd silently ordered her behind the counter. And she'd obeyed, recognizing his strength and responding to it.

He'd been a hero in the true sense of the word. He'd acted in a heroic way with no thought for his own safety. He hadn't had to come into the convenience store; he could have driven on or even considered himself a Good Samaritan by calling the police on his cell.

But he'd been a hero—*her* hero. And she couldn't stop thinking about him; her memories of this man were so incredibly vivid. She felt as if they'd been etched on her soul, she'd been so touched by his selfless actions.

Jen knew she was being unreasonable, thinking of this man, spinning thoughts about him, wondering if… Most likely he had a family, a wife and a couple of children. She wondered if they all knew how lucky they were to have a man like that in their lives to protect them.

For an instant, as she slid into the driver's seat and put her coffee and doughnuts down, she wished he was with her. She had a feeling if she could just lean on him for a few minutes, feel his arms around her, she wouldn't feel so afraid.

But that was impossible.

CODY KNEW HE HAD TO LEAVE the parking lot, but he couldn't seem to get his body in gear.

He was worn out. Perhaps *weary* was a better word. Soul sick, as his father would have said. He hadn't had a whole lot of energy when he'd started out this morning, and the robbery had finished him off.

But he knew he had to get to work, so he set himself a limit of ten more minutes. Then he opened the van's sliding side door and sat on the van's floor, facing outside with his booted feet on the cement. He took in deep breaths of the cool, morning desert air. It felt fresh and open. Vast and timeless.

For the first time in as long as he could remember, he felt glad to be alive.

JEN PULLED OUT OF THE PARKING lot, tried to take a sip of her coffee and found that she couldn't. Her hands were shaking that badly.

Setting the takeout cup in the Mustang's drink holder, she concentrated on driving through the small town, passing the first shopping center, driving by businesses and smaller, outlying houses surrounded by cacti and rock gardens. Trying to keep her attention on the road when her eyes were rapidly filling with frightened tears.

Aftershock. The shock was wearing off and she was starting to feel. And she didn't want to. At least not while she was driving.

She was in no shape to be on the road.

The motel she finally spotted was on the far side of town, a small, pale pink stucco affair with a tiled roof. The neon sign, complete with a cactus, was turned off. But all Jen cared about was the black-and-white Vacancy sign prominently displayed.

She pulled into the parking lot, went into the main office and got a room, then drove a few more spaces down so she was parked in front of door number seventeen. Taking her coffee, the doughnuts and her overnight bag, she locked her car, then unlocked the motel room's door and let herself in.

It was no resort, but the small room was pleasant. The queen-size bed had a clean, colorful green-and-cream-striped spread, and the room smelled fresh.

Locking the front door behind her, she dragged a ladder-back chair from the small table in front of the window and wedged it beneath the doorknob.

She knew this wasn't normal behavior on her part, but she found herself suddenly scared, wanting to make the room secure, not wanting to be caught off guard. And she also knew exactly where those fears were coming from and that they were very normal after what she'd just experienced.

Jen sat on the bed. She forced herself to sip her warm coffee, then take bites of the doughnuts, chew and swallow. Automatically. Again and again, even though she didn't really taste anything. She knew she had to go through these simple motions of living until she felt better again. Or at least until she got her blood sugar up.

The only thing she could compare the robbery to was a car accident she'd been in when she was sixteen. Her girlfriend had been driving when the car in front of them had gone completely out of control, smashing into the cement center divider. They'd plowed into the back of the runaway car. It had been over six months before she'd felt at ease in a car, either driving or as a passenger.

Now Jen knew it would take a while before she felt safe out in the world.

She stopped eating when the doughnuts and coffee threatened to come right back up, then walked into the motel bathroom. After a brief inspection of the small, utilitarian facilities, she turned on the shower, stripped off her clothing and reached for the wrapped bar of guest soap. It smelled of lemon.

If she closed her eyes, she could see the robber's expression, the way he'd looked at her as she'd slowly taken off her pink sweater.

More than anything, more than even wanting to feel safe again, she wanted to feel clean.

CODY KNEW HE'D BE LATE TO THE set if he didn't get it in gear. But his thoughts kept returning to the woman in the pink sweater. He wondered if she'd gotten to where she was going, if she had family waiting for her, a boyfriend or parents nearby. He wondered how she'd felt while being questioned by the police. He wondered if when she closed those extraordinary blue-gray eyes she saw the same images he did.

Forcing himself to finish the last of the lukewarm black coffee, he stretched, took a few deep breaths, then got into the van's driver's seat and turned on the ignition.

He drove through the desert town, intent on making good time until he passed a small, pink stucco motel and glimpsed that familiar candy-apple-red Mustang parked out front.

There couldn't be two cars with that particular paint job in a town this size.

Before he had time to question his judgement, he turned left, across the two-lane highway, into the motel's parking lot, and eased the battered van to a stop beside the sports car.

He stared at the motel room door. Door number seventeen. And as he studied that door, he knew that the woman with the gold bracelet was probably having as bad a time as he was. Worse, because she didn't look like the type to have been around guns for most of her life. Or lunatics.

Again he thought of the image she projected and the fact that she was traveling alone on the road. It just didn't fit. Women like her were cosseted and protected by their families, by their money. Not let loose on the road.

He thought of that red car and all the belongings piled in the backseat. Was she running away from someone? Did she need help? Whatever her life circumstances, having been caught in the middle of a robbery couldn't have helped things.

He sat in his van, staring at the motel door, knowing he was only postponing the inevitable. Something had pulled him toward this woman from the instant he'd seen her. Then they'd been thrown together and shared a pretty horrific experience. Now something was telling him to knock on that door and make sure she was all right.

He'd see how she was doing. Make sure she called

family, or at least had someone in her life who knew what had happened and could help her. Then he'd leave. But he had to see her, make sure she was all right. He had a feeling she was hurting and needed help.

He glanced away from the closed motel door, toward the red Mustang. Something about the woman made him want to protect her. Make life easier for her. He wanted to know who she was and where she was going. He wanted to talk to her. He couldn't let it alone.

Hell, he wanted to know her name.

Knowing he would do nothing to hurt her, acting on deep instinct, Cody opened the van door and got out. He slammed the door shut and locked it. Then he walked over to the motel room door and rapped on it sharply three times.

3

JEN WAS COMBING HER WET HAIR back from her face,
clad only in a short, ivory silk robe, when she heard
the three sharp knocks. The sounds made her jump.
She came up off the bed with her heart beating, her
hands once again shaking so much, she dropped the
blue wide-toothed comb.

She moved to the door, peered through the peep-
hole. And saw the man who had saved her life. Not
even hesitating, she moved the chair back, then
opened the door a crack, the chain still in place.

"Hello," he said.

"Hi." She didn't know why, but she was ridiculously glad to see him.

"You okay?" He got straight to the point, and she
had a feeling that this was his way.

She started to say yes—that automatic yes, that *Ev-
erything's fine* so often said to the question *How are
things going?* But her lips couldn't form the words.
She felt incapable of lying, of presenting that facade.
Instead she felt her mouth tremble. She trembled.
Her body felt as if it didn't belong to her.

She couldn't lie to this man. Though she hadn't
even known he existed a few hours ago, they had
been through too much together.

Life and death had a way of bonding people.

"No." The single word felt raw in her tight throat. She didn't offer any protest as he stepped closer.

"Take the chain off the door." That voice. So low and gentle, so soothing.

She did as he said, then seemed to watch from outside her own body as he opened the motel door further, stepped inside, closed it. He draped his jean jacket over one of the chairs, then he put his arm around her shoulders and steered her toward the bed. He sat her down on it and took her into his arms.

"Go ahead and cry," he said. "I may just join you."

His deep voice was all the persuasion she needed. The sobs came up now that she felt safe in the circle of his arms. Something about the way he held her made her feel so protected. No one could get her here, now. She wasn't alone; she was touching another human being—the only person who could truly understand what she'd been through during those terrible moments looking down the barrel of that shotgun.

She cried harder, remembering how he'd stumbled through the door, drawing the madman's gun, making sure it wasn't pointed at her. She cried because her first thought on seeing him had been that he was a useless drunk, another complication. Another problem. Instead he'd saved her life with no regard for his own.

Somehow she had to make him understand.

"I thought—I thought—" her words hiccupped on a sob "—you were drunk."

He continued to smooth her hair. He simply held her, offering no judgement concerning her crying, simply being there for her. It had been so long since anyone had truly been there for her, and Jen clung tighter. She couldn't let him go. Not yet. Not now.

"But when—when you came in—" She choked on another sob, and he patted her back as if she were an infant needing to be burped. Then he rubbed her back, his hands soothing, knowing exactly how to release the tightness. His touch both soothed and comforted. This man's touch was like none she'd ever felt before.

"I thought—I thought we were all going to die," she gasped out, fresh tears filling her eyes, running down her face.

"I know," he said. "Me, too."

Still those strong arms held her as she buried her face against his chest, her cheek smashed flat against his blue denim shirt. He smelled of coffee and sugar—the powdered sugar that had spilled on the front of his shirt. She held on tighter as she cried.

"Honey, honey," he said softly, his low voice almost crooning. "Tell me where your family is and I'll get you safely home. You shouldn't be alone—"

"No!" She clutched at his shirt harder, then, almost as if seeing herself and what she was doing for the first time, Jen felt embarrassment. Shame. She was out of control, in an anonymous motel room with a virtual stranger, dressed in nothing but a thin silk robe.

She pulled away slightly, gazed up at the man's face. *He doesn't feel like a stranger.*

She couldn't stop staring at him. Couldn't tear her gaze away. A dog barked somewhere in the distance. She heard the sound of a car drive by on the highway, then another. A door slammed.

She couldn't look away from him. The strong line of his jaw. His mouth. Those incredibly blue eyes.

Why had he been put in her path? No, not merely put there. *Flung* there. She remembered the way he'd stumbled into the convenience store and suddenly realized—

"You knew," she whispered. "Before you came in that door, you knew there was a robbery going down."

He tried to look away, as if embarrassed by what he'd done, but she slid her hand up, cupped the side of his face, held his gaze. Her fingers seemed to burn where she touched him, almost vibrate with energy, it felt so intense between them.

"You did."

He finally, almost reluctantly, nodded his head.

She continued to study him, knowing she would be able to see his face in her mind's eye for the rest of her life. Those eyes. The dark brown hair with that spark of auburn shot through it. The slight stubble on his chin. His strong, warm, muscular body.

But it was his eyes... Something about them haunted her. More than the slight redness, more than the weariness she saw there. She sensed something inside him had died or had very nearly been extinguished. She studied him, and he let her look until his own eyes filled and he glanced away. Over at the window. Down at the floor.

Anywhere, she knew, but at her.

She didn't know exactly how she came to the realization, but Jen knew he'd been ready to die for her and Johnny. Because this man who couldn't look at her felt there wasn't anything left for him. She'd seen it in his eyes. He was just marking time on this planet. He'd essentially kicked in that convenience store's door this morning and begun a death mission. He hadn't cared if he'd lived or died.

He'd saved her life, and now she knew he was suffering. A lost soul. And yet as lost as she sensed he was, he'd still helped her when that help had meant life and death to her. He'd still been a hero, his actions totally unselfish, his only thoughts to help her and Johnny survive that robbery.

She couldn't stand the fact that he'd done such a heroic thing and was now suffering for it.

"Oh, no," she whispered, stroking the side of his face with her fingertips. "No, don't feel that way."

He blinked, and it might have been as if those tears had never shimmered in his eyes. She watched as he slid the social mask into place. Almost like an actor's mask. And she wondered if anyone close to him knew how badly this man was hurting.

"No," she whispered, stroking the side of his face, then gently touching his split lip. Easing him back on the queen-size bed. Sliding beside him, all the while touching him. Her arms around him. Her body pressed against his. Simple human comfort. Simple touching. Letting him know he wasn't alone, she was with him. She would be with him now and help him through this.

He lay back beside her, his boots still on, fully dressed. She snuggled against him, her cheek on his chest, and felt his hands in her hair. Stroking her, sliding his fingers through the damp strands.

"I don't think either of us should be alone right

now," she said. How odd that she should recognize this stranger's despair. Probably because it was so close to her own. She shifted closer, held him. Listened until his breathing became deep and regular and she knew he had finally found solace in sleep.

Just before she drifted off, a thought flitted into consciousness.

How strange. I don't even know his name....

Then another.

But I do know him.... I do....

CODY CAME AWAKE ALMOST THREE hours later. It took him a few seconds to reorient himself, to remember how he'd come to this hotel room, to this time and place.

And this woman.

All of it came back to him, and he lay in bed, thankful to be alive. And thankful that this woman had been perceptive enough to know he was in no shape to hit the road.

He glanced at the bedside clock. He had just enough time to call Trevor and explain why he wouldn't be at work today. Trevor would have to shoot around him, but unless Cody made that call, the director would believe he was out there, coming off a bender. The best thing he could do was clean up and be on time tomorrow, ready for work.

But he had to call him.

Cody reached for his jacket, found his cell phone and punched in the number. He waited, hoping to get Trevor directly but getting the director's voice mail instead. At the beep Cody left a message, swiftly and succinctly explaining why he wouldn't be on the set today. He told Trevor about the robbery attempt but asked him not to say anything to anyone. Then he made his apologies and hung up.

Perhaps he'd go to his director's hotel room tonight when he returned and apologize for holding him up. He probably could have really pushed and made it back to the set, but intuition told him not to leave this woman alone today.

He eased himself out of bed, then looked down at the sleeping woman, her hair spread out around her head like a blond halo. She lay curled on her side in the large bed, the silky robe barely covering her. They'd both fallen asleep on top of the coverlet. Now he studied her, that fall of silky blond hair, those slender, perfect legs.

After a moment he eased the bedspread, blanket and top sheet down, then tucked her in. The air-conditioning in the motel room had kicked in as it had gotten hotter outside, and he didn't want her to catch a chill.

He settled the bedding around her shoulders, up to her chin, and she snuggled deeper into the bed in sleep, then smiled. He watched her face, committing it to memory.

That hair. He'd loved touching it. Comforting her. And he wondered again how a woman so delicate came to be out on the road by herself. There was a piece to this puzzle he didn't have or understand.

Yet for all that her appearance said she was delicate, she had a spine there, as well. She'd responded to his unspoken command back at the robbery site.

She hadn't gone all hysterical or fallen apart until they'd been alone together in this motel room.

She would get through this. He was just thankful he could help her along.

She was also perceptive as hell, and that scared him a little, if he were honest with himself. She'd looked at him, and within minutes of their being alone, she'd seen far more than all the tabloids and newspapers, than all the reporters and talk-show hosts had ever noticed.

She'd seen him. And she hadn't been afraid.

Cody closed his eyes and took a deep breath, considering how he felt. His legs felt a whole lot more solid beneath him. Just that short amount of sleep and that human touch, that contact, had grounded him. He remembered reading an article that had said sleep was the brain's way of organizing and making sense of data, and the short nap he'd taken with—

He didn't even know her name.

Cody smiled down at the sleeping woman. The short nap he'd taken with this angel had allowed him to make sense of some pretty horrific data. As his mother had always said, things look a whole lot better after a solid meal and a good night's sleep.

And, in his case, a shower.

Not wanting to disturb her, he moved as quietly as possible, picking up the blue comb at the foot of the bed as he headed toward the small bathroom.

Small wasn't the right word. *Miniscule* was. And already crowded with her toiletries. Just enough room for a toilet, a sink and a shower. He was a big man and would barely have room to turn around in the small shower stall.

So as not to crowd it even further, Cody swiftly took off his boots and peeled off his clothing just outside the door. Entering the bathroom, he closed the door gently, then turned on the shower, already anticipating the feel of hot water on his tense shoulders.

The water was good and hot and plentiful. The small sliver of guest soap was lemon-scented, and he used a generous amount, lathering it over his body, feeling as if he were washing away the scent of fear, washing away all that had happened just that morning.

He ducked his head beneath the sharp, hot spray, then used some of the woman's shampoo. It had an herbal smell, not too bad. Cody rinsed his hair, enjoying the feel of the hot water working the tension out of his body.

Outside the shower, standing by the sink with a white towel around his waist, he risked one more loan. One that was more personal but necessary. He searched through her toiletry bag until he found a plastic razor. Lathering up with the lemon-scented soap, he shaved, swiping away at the weekend stubble covering the lower half of his face.

When he finished, he wiped his face with a hot, wet washcloth, then combed his clean hair with the blue comb he'd found at the foot of the bed.

Feeling pleased with the way he looked and feeling so much better, confident that he could drive back to the set without breaking down, all he needed now was a good meal. Perhaps he could ask this woman—after making sure he finally found out what her name was—if she'd join him.

Opening the bathroom door and letting a rush of cool air into the steam-filled room, he stepped outside. Cody wished for just an instant that he had clean clothing to put on. Then he let the white motel towel that had been draped around his hips fall to the floor.

Just before he reached for his worn jeans, he felt a sudden jolt of awareness and glanced up.

She was awake. And watching him.

HE WAS THE MOST BEAUTIFUL man she'd ever seen.

Tall, strong and muscular. Powerful shoulders. Perfectly proportioned. She could see defined muscles in his legs and chest, even his abdomen. And his chest was covered with a sprinkling of dark hair.

Her heart in her throat, Jen looked up at his face.

He blushed, the reddish hue suffusing his face and neck.

She couldn't imagine why—until she glanced down at his body again and saw he was becoming swiftly and gloriously aroused. His sex, as impressive as the rest of his body, was lengthening. Thickening.

Again, he was the most beautiful man she'd ever seen.

She'd awakened at the tail end of his shower, coming to consciousness while hearing the steady, soft fall of water. Then she'd smiled seeing how he'd tucked her in while she'd slept. The tenderness and intimacy of the gesture had touched her deeply.

She'd known he was taking a shower in her motel room, and it hadn't bothered her a bit. She, a woman who hadn't let her own fiancé touch her intimately until they'd been together for over a year, felt perfectly comfortable with this almost total stranger taking a shower in her motel room while she lay in a queen-size bed clad only in a whisper-thin silk robe.

She didn't know why, but there weren't as many barriers between them. Or maybe she did. Maybe she'd gone through most of her life having perfected the rather distant, cool and collected social face and manner that her father deemed appropriate. And maybe she'd set out on this journey to the West Coast because a part of her—the wisest part—knew her life was slowly killing her.

Maybe she wanted to live. To really feel alive. To know what that felt like after having come so close to dying.

But she couldn't take her eyes off him. That muscular, masculine body. That large, strong erection. When he bent down and reached for his jeans, she said just one word.

"No."

Though she'd spoken softly, the word sounded loud in the quiet of the motel room. It stilled his movement for his clothing. He looked at her, disbelieving. Puzzled. But also desiring her. He couldn't hide it any more than she could.

But Jen knew he wouldn't join her on her bed unless she let him know that was exactly what she wanted. This man, this stranger, wasn't the type to take advantage of a woman. But she wouldn't have wanted him or felt as safe with him if he'd been that sort of man.

He hadn't seemed to register what she'd said, and Jen realized words were not the answer. Actions were. She'd told him, but now she would show him exactly what she wanted.

Sitting up in bed, she slipped the ivory silk robe off her shoulders, letting it slide to her waist. She felt the cool, air-conditioned air in the motel room against her breasts. As she looked down at them, unable to look at him, she felt her nipples harden into tight little points of sensation.

She wet her lips, trying to find the words to tell him what she wanted. Her throat felt dry, constricted with both a sort of fear and an equal amount of excitement. And somehow she knew this was right, knew this was what she wanted and what he needed.

In the end she merely looked up and held out her hand, knowing he could see exactly what she was trying to tell him in her eyes. It had to be there—emotions this strong had to come out somehow. A part of her couldn't believe this was really happening, that she was making this happen, but a stronger feeling told her that this was right, it had to happen.

The connection, that strange electric sensation when she'd touched his cheek, remained. Slowly he crossed the room. Then he knelt down on the bed as she slid down on the soft mattress, onto her back. She closed her eyes as she felt his fingers swiftly untie the sash of her short robe, then lifted her hips as he yanked it away.

She opened her eyes, watched him as he studied her for a long moment, looking at her body almost as if he couldn't believe what was about to happen. What had to happen.

Their eyes met. Held. She knew he was giving her one last chance to back out, to reconsider, even though she could see he was poised and ready, tense with need, his sex swollen and full, painfully aroused.

But this was more than mere sex. She was acting on pure instinct, wanting to reaffirm life in the most primal, instinctual manner possible. After coming so close to death, she wanted to feel again, to know she was alive. She wanted to be close to him, as close as one person could get to another.

She wanted to take him into her body and offer him peace. She wanted to fully experience her own sexuality, which had never happened before. And Jen knew it would happen with this man. She felt more when he simply touched her than when other men had been inside her, moving, the sensation not horrible, simply...*pleasant.*

Pleasant was not a word she'd ever use in connection with her sexual feelings toward this man. It wouldn't be pleasant with this man, it would be something far more than that.

I want you, she thought, *like I've never wanted another man in my life.* She reached up, her gaze never leaving his, knowing that with a single touch she would set something in motion. Something that felt as if it had always been meant to be. Destiny. Kismet. Whatever you wanted to call it.

One touch. One leap of faith. She only knew she had to take it, because he was making this her decision, he was giving her complete control.

Her hand came up, and it was steady. She touched the side of his face, now smooth. He'd shaved.

At her touch he seemed to shudder, and she saw he'd been holding himself in check for her. She smiled at him, knowing that smile was reflected in her eyes, and he turned his face and kissed her palm.

Sensation, electric and hot, shot all the way through her body. To her breasts, then lower, pooling between her thighs. Making her ache. She'd never felt this way with any other man and knew she never would.

She wanted this moment as she'd never wanted anything else in her life. She was being given something few women experienced in their lifetime and she wanted to take it. Her hand slipped around the back of his neck as she urged him closer, pulled him down on top of her. Their naked skin touched all along their bodies. She barely had time to cry out at the wonder of it, how it felt, before his lips came down over hers. His body covered hers. He moved between her thighs. And she simply surrendered to something that felt so right.

And for the first time since early this morning, that horrible morning when she'd thought she was going to die, Jen felt alive.

4

HE'D NEVER FELT MORE WELCOMED into a woman's bed. More wanted. When she'd held out her hand to him, looking small and delicate in the middle of the large bed, his heart had opened, started to ache. And feelings he hadn't felt in a long time had begun their long, arduous climb to the surface.

He'd sensed what she was offering him was more than a mere physical sensation or release. It felt as if he were being handed a lifeline. And he took it. He'd never wanted anything more. He took it and followed her down onto the bed in the middle of the day. Life might be going on all around them, but for this day, this hour, this moment, they were alone in the quiet coolness of this motel room, with just each other and the strong emotion that seemed to flow between them so effortlessly.

When he kissed her, it didn't seem like the first time, they fit together so well. She seemed familiar to him in the best possible way, and he deepened the kiss, feeling his body quicken, hoping that it would not betray him or shame him.

He wanted her with the intensity of a teenage boy, that strong hunger and desire, but he wanted to give her the skill and knowledge of a man who knew how to love a woman thoroughly. Yet all of his desire, his emotions, seemed to be demanding he get as close as possible as quickly as possible.

He broke the kiss and, though he wasn't usually a man who talked in bed, whispered, "Your name." He wanted to know her name.

"Jennifer." The one word came out on a sigh, so deeply satisfied, and it thrilled him to hear that tone in her voice when all he'd done was kiss her.

"Jen," he said with a deep sense of satisfaction, and something flickered in those deep blue-gray eyes.

"What is it?" he whispered, looking down at her. His body was pressed into hers, even though he was taking most of his weight on his forearms.

She smiled up at him with a hint of tentativeness. "I like the way you say my name."

"Is Jennifer better? Jenny?"

"Jen's fine. You?"

It took him a moment to get that she was asking him his name. "Cody. Cody Roberts."

There was the slightest flicker of awareness in her expression, and he prayed she wouldn't suddenly recognize who he was and what he did. He'd had enough of those kinds of encounters—women who slept with him to get close to success or to get a part in one of his films. Or just to say they'd slept with a star. Even a fallen star.

"It feels like…I know the name."

His whole body tensed.

"It must be because," she whispered, "I feel so close to you."

He didn't want to talk. He wanted to kiss her. He wanted to make love to her, to make it good for her, to lose himself inside her. In his experience, you were either attracted to a woman or you weren't, and he was incredibly attracted to this woman.

"Jen," he whispered. Then he kissed her.

SHE'D NEVER FELT THIS WAY with any other man.

It wasn't as if she had a vast amount of sexual experience. She'd had only a couple of boyfriends in college and then Ethan. Ethan, who her father had practically handpicked for her and for whom she had felt absolutely nothing.

Ethan, who was waiting back in Chicago for her, even though she'd broken their engagement and given him back the flawless diamond ring before she'd started on her trip to California and freedom.

Her father had thought she was insane. By implication, so had Ethan. But Jen had known there was something else or someone else out there for her. She'd known that the life she would have had with Ethan would have gone precisely, step-by-step, according to her father's master plan for an ordered life.

It would have been an emotional jail cell. A gilded cage. And she would have beaten her wings frantically against the bars, and no one would have heard. But the end result would have been the same.

Now she had a chance to fly free. To live.

She was glad as she looked up at Cody that no one would ever know about this encounter. She wanted it for herself alone, didn't want anyone judging her or giving her any unwelcome and unasked-for opinions.

No one would ever know about the robbery other than the police and perhaps the local news. Certainly no one she knew. She would have this time alone, out of time, all for herself. She would give to Cody and, in giving to him, find out so much about herself.

She'd left Chicago because she'd been afraid she'd stopped feeling anything, and since she'd met this man she'd done nothing but feel.

She touched his lip. "Does it hurt?"

"No."

She smiled. "Then kiss me," she whispered. "Kiss me again."

He smiled down at her, and her heart sped up at the look in those dark blue eyes. "You're really something," he whispered, then kissed the side of her neck. "I didn't come here thinking this was going to happen."

"I know." She hesitated. "I didn't open the door thinking something like this would happen."

That smile. Devastating. He kissed her temple and whispered, "Sure? Are you okay, Jenny?"

"Never better."

He laughed, a low, satisfied sound that thrilled her, then she ran her fingers through his hair and gently tugged his head down to hers, his mouth to hers. And then one kiss blended into the next and the next, and her body began to soften, to become pliant and willing and so filled with yearning.

She was more than ready when he touched her breasts, when he moved down and kissed them, took them into his mouth and pulled on them strongly. Almost blind with need, her eyes shut, she arched up against him, all feeling centered where his hands and mouth were touching her.

And she couldn't stop touching the strong, hard muscles beneath his smooth, hot skin. Her hands were restless, taking him in, learning him, wanting to commit him to tactile memory.

Before, she'd felt a subtle impatience from her partners, as if they felt she wasn't quite keeping up with them, as if they were indulging her by going slowly. Now she felt as if she were racing ahead of Cody, on fire, impatient for what he was going to do next, wanting more and more and more….

When his hand slipped between her thighs and cupped her, she was almost ashamed at how ready she was. He looked at her as he touched her and saw the bright flush on her face.

"Don't," he whispered, sliding back up and kissing her softly. "Don't go there, Jen."

Her face was so hot, it prickled. She wasn't at all surprised he read her mood. That short moment when he'd first come into the room and they'd sat on the edge of the bed had told her he was a sensitive man.

"Don't stop, Cody," she whispered. "Please…"

He did as she asked but kept his gaze on her face as she felt first one finger, then a second, gently push her open, move within her, stretching her, readying her—

"Oh!" The sensation that caught hold was a new one, and she looked up at him and saw a smile in his eyes.

"Yes," he whispered, then kissed her hard, his hand relentless, his fingers so knowing, the sensations so strong, she closed her eyes, tilted her head back into the soft pillow—

And cried out as she came, her thighs falling open in the aftermath, her body first tense and then so wonderfully relaxed. She felt as if she were melting into the mattress as she turned toward him. Her hands trembled as she grasped his hard shoulders, seeking stability after having her sensual foundation rocked.

This was what had been missing. What had seemed like a hopeless amount of work with any other partner had come so naturally with this man.

"Mmm," she sighed against his neck. Then she smiled as she felt him start to laugh.

"So, I'm funny?" she whispered. She'd never opened the front curtains when she'd first come in, and now with the only light coming from the open bathroom door, the room was dimly lit, like twilight. Not dark but not light either.

"No," he whispered, pulling her more strongly into his arms. "Not funny at all."

She opened her eyes and looked up at him. He was studying her with an intent expression on his face.

She touched that strong jawline once again, loving the feel of it on her fingertips.

"Let me give to you," she whispered.

"It works both ways, Jenny," he said. "We give to each other."

"But I haven't—"

"You will." He took her hand, guided it right to where he wanted it, taught her how to please him. And she found that it wasn't awkward as it had been in the past. She wanted to please him, wanted to make this good for him. It thrilled her that she had it in her power to excite him to this extent.

She was practically shaking with reaction when he finally rolled her over onto her back and slid between her spread thighs. And while she'd thought there might be a moment of discomfort when their bodies joined together, when that moment came, her body opened and she accepted all of him in one smooth, hard thrust.

He began to move inside her, strong strokes that seemed to burn their way up inside her, exciting her. She held on to him, grasped his forearms, his shoulders, wrapped her legs around his body tightly because she felt as if at any second she might come apart and fly off their bed.

And again, that racing toward completion, that tightening pressure deep within, then—

She came with a low, anguished moan, and he followed her, finding his own release, pushing into her and then, with strong contractions of his own, finishing.

She felt his muscular chest rising and falling, heard his labored breathing, ran her hands up his damp back and had never in all of her adult life felt closer to another living person.

She kissed the side of his face and he sighed, and the sound seemed to move his body even closer to her.

"Am I too heavy?" he whispered, and she smiled against his neck.

"No." She'd never felt more satisfied in her life. "No. Stay right where you are."

"Hmm."

They stayed that way for long moments, until Cody finally eased off her. But he kept his arms around her the entire time, pulling her tightly against him. She breathed in his scent, felt totally safe in his arms and so relaxed after her own release.

Satiated, content, feeling there was no place in the world she'd rather be, Jen drifted off to sleep.

SHE AWAKENED SLOWLY. THE motel room was dark, the only light a small sliver that came from the partially closed bathroom door. Cody must have gotten up and flicked on the light over the mirror at some point.

She turned her head and found him lying next to her, wide-awake. Her eyes had adjusted to the dark, and she saw that he was looking at her. He must have been watching her sleep.

"How do you feel?" he said, his voice so gentle.

"Wonderful."

"Really?"

She could hear the skepticism in his voice. This man could read her too well.

"Wonderful about you," she said softly. "Not so good about everything else. About this morning, I mean."

"You need to talk it out."

She shifted closer to him in the big bed. "What do you mean?"

"Jen, do you trust me?"

"Yes."

"I used to do some work with people who experienced trauma. It was right after a pretty rough time in my life. And I learned a method of…kind of debriefing people after they'd been through something like what we went through this morning."

She considered this. "How does it help?"

"You ask the question, they talk and they get it all out. It helps to release it and to get it out within a short time of the actual incident. I'm not saying it will fix it entirely, but it goes a long way toward making it better."

"Okay."

He took her hand, his fingers interlacing with hers, and she was grateful for his strength. "I'll answer the questions right after you do. It'll help me, as well."

"So we'll be doing this together," she said.

"Yes."

"Good."

"Jen, where were you when the incident first occurred?"

"Getting a cup of coffee and some doughnuts in a convenience store." As she said the words, she could picture herself at the scene. She pulled the covers up over her bare shoulders with her free hand.

"Outside in the parking lot, looking at the front of the store," Cody said, answering the same question. Then he asked, "What first concerned you?"

This was hard. Jen could feel the painful memories surge up, and she resisted the self-protective instinct to push them down, ignore them.

"I thought—I thought I was going to die."

Cody's hand squeezed hers, and he continued to both ask and answer the specific set of questions.

"BETTER?" HE SAID ONCE THEY were finished.

"I do feel a lot better." She'd answered all the questions he'd put to her. It had felt as if she'd been experiencing it all over again, but this time she'd had Cody right with her. She'd shared it with him, as he had with her. And in the process felt closer to him than ever.

He smiled. "Great." He cupped her cheek with one hand, then kissed her gently. "I'm not saying you still won't experience a lot of emotions, but they shouldn't be as severe because you—and I—were both able to talk them out. Just take it easy for the next few weeks and take good care of yourself."

"I will." Her stomach chose that exact moment to rumble.

Cody laughed softly. "Do you want to go out and get some food or something?"

"Later," she said, moving across the short expanse of bed that separated them. His hand grasped her waist in response and she came alive at his touch. He smoothed his fingers down over her hip, then up until he was cupping one breast.

She didn't want to think about where this was going or if it was meant to go anyplace at all. She'd wanted this moment out of time and she was going to make the most of it.

"Jen," he said softly, then took her hand and showed her how much he wanted her. Strong and sure and hard, his body didn't lie. And that physical truth thrilled her.

She leaned back on her pillow, her gaze never leaving his. "Come here," she said, reveling in this newfound sense of feminine power.

He laughed and moved closer.

"WHAT KIND OF PIZZA DO YOU like?" he whispered into the darkness after they'd both had enough time to recuperate.

"Vegetarian?"

"You're not sure?"

She had to laugh at how tentative her answer had sounded. "I'm not sure if you're a big meat eater or not."

"We could do mushroom," he said. "Do you like black olives?"

"Yeah."

"Onions?" he said. "Peppers?"

"No," she said, hoping their evening was still far from over.

"I'll be right back," he said, getting out of her bed and walking unselfconsciously toward his pile of clothing. He slipped into his jeans and began to shrug into his shirt.

"I can come with," she offered.

"You stay right there and rest," he said, and she loved the devilish twinkle in his eyes. "I have plans for you."

THEY ATE DINNER NAKED, sprawled out in bed. Neither of them wanted the television on, not wanting to see any local news report of today's robbery.

"You're so neat," he said midway through their impromptu meal. "There's not a crumb on the sheets."

"That's bad?" she said, teasing him.

"Nah. I guess I'm just a slob."

They finished their pizza. He'd also brought her a salad. And the place he'd gone had apparently also had very good Italian coffee, because he'd brought her a latte with four extra sugars.

"How did you know?" she said as she ripped open the packets and poured them into her coffee.

"You seem like a sweet sort of person," he said, smiling.

Sipping her coffee, with the white bed sheet wrapped around her, she said, "Where did you come from, Cody Roberts?"

"What do you mean?"

"Why were you up so early and heading for a convenience store?"

"Just getting some coffee on my way to work." He hesitated, then said, "Where's that family of yours?"

"Chicago."

He was silent for a moment, then said, "You going to tell them what happened?"

"Nope. And it's not 'them.' It's just my father."

She could tell Cody was watching her as she stirred her coffee.

"Your old man finds out about the robbery and you can kiss this trip goodbye, is that it?"

"Something like that."

He was silent again, but she was pleased to discover that the small moments of silence between them weren't uncomfortable.

"Is there a boyfriend in the picture?"

"No."

"Did you leave someone behind, back in Chicago?"

"Yes. But it was over before I left." She decided to be daring and reach for what she wanted. "You?"

"No. No one."

The knowledge that he was a single man made her feel light. Happier than she'd been in a while. But she cautioned herself, not wanting to make more of this than it was. Perhaps for Cody it was just a one-night stand, something he would think about at odd moments in his life.

The moment she had the thought, she rejected it. Having been denied intimacy for a great deal of her life, having been used to long periods of loneliness, she knew what they had was special. Jen didn't think she was deluding herself.

"I'm glad," she said.

"You are?"

"Yes." She took a deep breath. "You don't seem the sort of man who would cheat on his girlfriend. Or his wife."

He'd brought back a coffee for himself, as well, and she noticed that he took it black. The Italian coffee smelled heavenly.

"Where are you going?" he said after a while.

"Los Angeles."

"Do you have family there?"

"A girlfriend," she said. "Maria. She runs a coffeehouse on Melrose Avenue. She said I could come and stay with her. I'm going to wait tables for a while until I decide what it is I want to do."

"So you're in transit," he said, sitting up and adjusting the pillows behind him.

"You?"

"Kind of the same. Finishing up a job, then not sure what I'll be doing next."

"Do you like what you do?"

"It has its moments," he said. "But after I'm done, I'll be heading back to Los Angeles." Those blue eyes, so direct, so intent on her, warmed her, softened her.

"Small world," she said and took another sip of her coffee.

"I'd like to see you again."

The way he was so direct impressed her. No, it excited her. And she knew at that moment that her instincts had been correct and she would see this man again.

"I'd like that," she said, looking directly at him. She'd played so many coy little games in Chicago, being a lady, remembering "who you are," as her father had always said. The only problem with that was that the men in her life had always treated her like a lady and never realized she was a woman.

"Can I get your phone number?"

Happiness threatened to bubble out of her. "I'll give you my cell number and the number of Maria's coffeehouse. It's called A Bit of a Buzz."

"I've seen it. I know where it is, right around Melrose and Gardner, on the…the south side of the street."

"That's it," she said, impressed. She'd flown out last January to help Maria open her business, to support her friend. And watching how excited her friend was about launching her own business, she'd realized how empty her own life was. The seeds of her plan to escape had been planted that weekend.

She gave him the numbers, watched the way he wrote them both down and then folded the piece of motel stationery and put it inside his wallet.

"I'll be back in town in about three weeks, six at the most. But I'll call you."

"I'd like that." She took the last sip of her coffee and set the empty cup down on her bedside table. "Thank you for dinner."

"My pleasure. I should have taken you out."

"This was better."

"What do you want now?" he said, and she knew he was letting her set the pace their evening would take. In the morning she'd be on the road, and so would he.

But he had her number.

"Could we sleep a little more?" she said, hoping he would understand.

"Sure." He slid across the sheets toward her, took her in his arms and they lay like spoons. She closed her eyes, feeling safe again, and before she took ten breaths, she had fallen asleep, exhausted.

DELAYED REACTION TO THE stress, Cody thought as he lay next to Jen, listening to her sleep. It was obvious that she'd led a much more sheltered life than he had. This whole day had to have hit her with the force of a runaway truck.

He closed his eyes, felt his body finally relax. Something about this woman gave him a sense of peace. She was comfortable to be around, easy to be with. And at the same time she aroused him. A nice combination.

He was glad that what he did for a living hadn't come up. He didn't want to appear as a loser in her eyes, and the moment she connected him with *the* Cody Roberts, action-adventure hero who had blown his movie career to hell and back with bad behavior, she might have second thoughts about seeing him again.

Then again, she might trust who he really was, who he had shown her he was.

The last thing in the world he'd been looking for was a relationship with a woman. He'd felt over the last several months that he barely had his own life under control. The idea of a relationship had been months away on his master plan.

It was strange how they were both in the process of reinventing their lives. She was moving out to the West Coast, he was attempting to get his career back on track. And then the robbery this morning, and they'd been thrown in each other's path.

Cody smiled into the darkness, feeling Jen's warmth against his body. Funny how the world worked. In his experience, whether you were ready for something or not, the world generally gave you exactly what you needed.

And he knew he needed Jen.

There was something different about her, something that set her apart from any woman he'd ever met. Cody knew, whether he was ready or not, he wasn't going to let her out of his life. If she wanted to have a relationship with him, he was ready to give it his all. It was up to Jen. And in his eyes, he'd be a lucky man if her decision was yes.

His mind was running away with him again. He shifted farther down into the bed, pulled the covers up more tightly around him and made sure Jen was securely tucked in.

Then he slept.

SHE WOKE IN THE MIDDLE OF THE night and knew he was awake behind her. Turning in his arms, she moved into his warmth, searching for his mouth with her own, kissing him even as she reached down and stroked his arousal. She'd felt its pressure against her backside as they'd spooned, but now she gently pushed him until he was lying on his back. Then those strong arms came around her waist and lifted her until she was astride him, taking him all the way in, then moving on him with total abandon.

He'd left the bathroom light on, and there was just enough light so they could see each other. He reached for her breast, and she gasped as his other large hand splayed out on her back and urged her down so he could pleasure her with his mouth. She pushed down more urgently on him, rode him hard with a desperate sexual urgency, until she felt him start to thrust wildly, seeking release.

He came then, before she did, but once he'd rested for a very short time, he proved he was more than up to the challenge of more lovemaking. This time, flat on her back with her legs up around his shoulders, he thrust into her so deeply and strongly that she practically screamed when she came.

"You can make noise," he whispered roughly, almost as if he sensed she was holding back.

Years of repression warred with intense sensual desire. When she peaked, she bit his shoulder to stifle the noise.

Afterward she said, "I was afraid someone would complain."

He laughed softly in the darkness. "Not about that kind of noise. Anyone who heard that, if they were honest, would wish they were doing exactly what we were doing."

SHE CAME AWAKE EARLY THE NEXT morning to the feel of him stroking her body softly, her belly and breasts, her buttocks. She was more than ready for him, and when he was deep inside her and whispered, "Someday we're going to do this in a place where you can scream your head off," it sent her over the edge.

When she came back to consciousness, out of a brief, voluptuous sleep, he was standing over her, showered and fully dressed.

He sat down on the bed as she started to struggle up. "No," he said softly. "Stay right that way. I want to remember this picture." So she stayed, lying back against the pillows, the sheets twisted and tangled, exposing one of her breasts to his gaze.

"Cody," she said, linking her hand with his, entwining their fingers tightly together. "Thank you."

"Thank *you*," he said, then leaned over and kissed her hard. She went into his arms and he held her for a long time. And she was the one to move away—a new experience for her. Her father rarely hugged her and had always broken away first.

"Jen," he said, cupping her chin in his palm. "I'll call you. And I'll come see you the minute I'm back in Los Angeles."

"Okay." Now that he was leaving, for some insane reason she was already missing him.

"Don't get that worried look on your face. I'm not like most guys. When I say I'll call you, I will."

"Okay." She hesitated. "One more kiss?"

He lowered himself down on her bed, kissed her once, then twice, then again and again. She threaded her fingers through his hair, caressed his cheek—

"Aw, hell!" he said as he kicked off his boots. "But then I've really got to go."

"I know," she said, smiling up at him as he swiftly unbuttoned his shirt. It was just as hard for him to leave her as it was for her to know he was walking away.

And that was good.

5

THE SOUND OF A CAR HORN blaring in the parking lot woke Jen up. Lying in the motel bed, the covers pulled up over her head, it took her a moment to remember where she was. Then she rolled over in bed and eyed the clock on the bedside table. Ten fifty-eight. She'd slept a little after Cody had left. She stretched, then lay back among the rumpled bedding.

Guilt didn't have a chance to enter into her thought process. She didn't regret a moment. She'd known there was something sexual in life she hadn't experienced, some deep connection in lovemaking that had eluded her.

Until yesterday, with Cody.

Strange how sometimes the most horrible things also contained the seeds of something wonderful. If anyone had asked her if she'd wanted to be caught in the middle of a robbery, the answer would have been an unequivocal no.

But if she hadn't been in that store, been through those moments when she thought she and Johnny were going to die, she might not have met Cody. And she might not have been in a frame of mind to let things progress as swiftly as they had.

Because she'd faced death, she'd also wanted to embrace life. The urge had been powerful and primal, and she'd chosen to be swept along in the intensity of its wake. She'd wanted to feel alive.

Regret didn't even enter into it.

She slid out of bed and went toward the small bathroom. She had just enough time to shower and pack up her things before checking out and hitting the road. Now more than ever she wanted to reach Los Angeles and start her new life. There wasn't a moment to waste.

WHEN CODY RETURNED TO THE set, Trevor was all smiles.

The fifty-something British director wasn't too cynical, but he'd been in the entertainment business long enough to have a profound understanding of the way it sometimes worked. He accepted it and had that rare quality which enabled him to thrive as a creative artist in one of the most powerful and difficult businesses in the world.

He'd been discovered in his late twenties, after shooting a series of extremely inventive car commercials in London that had garnered industry respect. A few feature films swiftly followed—opportunities he'd taken and run with as he'd moved to Los Angeles. The third had been a monster hit, and Trevor Mac-Farland had been on his way. He'd never looked back.

He was doing this film as a favor for an old friend who'd left the project after suffering a sudden severe heart attack. The producers had been relieved because Trevor was known to be a director who brought in a picture on time and usually under budget.

He didn't suffer fools and didn't let leading men or ladies get away with any of the craziness that could jeopardize a picture. Trevor ran a tight ship, and everyone knew it.

With his gray hair, full beard and lively green eyes, he looked like an elf. His five-foot-six stature and slender build accentuated this first impression. Now those eyes expressed several emotions: kindness, compassion and concern.

"Cody," he said as he saw him, and Cody braced himself for the criticism that was sure to come.

It never did.

"Trevor," he began, only to have the director hold up a hand, effectively silencing him.

"We all know what you did," he said.

For one awful moment Cody thought of the motel room he'd shared with Jen, the intimacy and peace he'd found there, along with that intense sexual excitement. How could Trevor have found out? How could anyone have known?

"The robbery," Trevor continued. "At that convenience store. It made the morning news."

"What?" His mind didn't seem to want to function. He'd told Trevor about the robbery on his cell phone, but the idea that what had happened had made the local news was something he hadn't expected.

"Someone at the *National Star* got hold of the footage from the security camera after it aired this morning. You were recognized. They have people they pay everywhere, you know. So they bought it, along with exclusive rights to air it. A little of it, a teaser, was played on the news this morning. The rest is going to premiere on their show tonight and for the following nights, bits of it stretched over this next week, stringing it out until the very end." His smile was wry. This was how their world worked, and Trevor accepted it. "You're a hero, Cody."

For a long moment Cody took all of it in. It was one thing for his personal life to be invaded, scrutinized under a microscope, served up for public consumption. He'd come into this life by his own choice as an actor, a celebrity, and knew that this came with the territory.

He'd gone through an extremely rough time after his father had died, and in his absolute grief he'd gone on some very public drinking and partying binges. Anything to dull the emotional pain. The press had indulged him at first, called him the bad boy gone wild. But when he hadn't snapped out of it, they'd crucified him.

His career had been all but over before he'd auditioned for this film, accepting a much lower salary than he normally did for the privilege of working again.

He'd learned some hard lessons over the last three years. Long ago he'd accepted the way this business worked; it came with being an actor. But Jen...

"One of the producers heard about it this morning."

The sinking feeling in Cody's stomach intensified.

"One of his people here on the set must have called. What could be more perfect in their eyes than an action hero who actually saves a couple of lives?" Trevor didn't say this unkindly. He was simply a man who understood the realities of the business. It was one of the reasons he'd worked steadily for almost thirty years.

Cody had no answer.

"The point is, he was delighted. In his mind, now there's all this attention and publicity focused on his film, and what could be better than that?"

The only thing Cody could think of was what would happen to Jen. And Johnny. Would their lives be thrown into turmoil?

"Are you all right?" Trevor said. The words were spoken with genuine concern. Another reason Trevor MacFarland's career had been so successful over the years was that he genuinely liked people, knew how to work with them and made the effort to understand his actors. While he tolerated no nonsense on his sets, he treated everyone with the utmost respect.

"Yeah." Cody ran his hand through his hair, then eyed the director. "Yeah, I'm okay."

"Are you going to be able to work today?"

He made the decision in a heartbeat. "Yes."

"Good." The director studied him for a moment, then said again, "Good." He hesitated. "What about that girl? And the clerk? How did they handle it?"

"As well as could be expected."

"It's a horrific thing to go through," Trevor said. "I was held up at gunpoint one night in New York. The entire thing took only a few minutes, but it seemed like forever while it was happening. It took me a while to get over it."

"I know the feeling," Cody said.

"Work always helps," Trevor said. "But if you

need anything or feel as if something isn't right, let me know immediately. Understood?"

"Yes." Cody hesitated. When their first director had left suddenly, he'd thought the film was cursed. Then Trevor had stepped on board, and the man had been a godsend. He was a real human being in a business that attracted all sorts of people for many reasons, not all of them good.

"Okay." Trevor reached his hand up to Cody's shoulder, squeezed briefly, then stepped back, his hand dropping to his side.

"Thank you, Trevor."

"Take care of yourself, Cody. It's the only life you have. And get Kim to take a look at that lip."

WHEN JEN CHECKED OUT OF THE motel just before noon, the girl behind the desk couldn't stop staring at her, a speculative gleam in her brown eyes.

The motel clerk looked as if she were still in high school, with her honey-blond hair pulled off her face in a ponytail and the smattering of freckles on her cute upturned nose. As she handed Jen her receipt, Jen wondered why she was the object of such curiosity.

She answered the question that yes, everything had been wonderful, and was ready to leave when the clerk whispered, "Oh my God, you're the girl who was in that robbery yesterday!"

Jen stopped then and said, "What are you talking about?" hoping she could buy some time.

"The video. They played part of the security video from that convenience store robbery on the news this morning, the very beginning of the whole thing, and then they told us what happened afterward, all about Cody and how he rescued the two of you! And they're going to show the entire video later in the week!"

Jen couldn't control the sinking feeling in the pit of her stomach. The media had gotten hold of the security tape and were using it shamelessly, as if it were Sweeps Week for the major networks.

The girl, not noticing her reaction, kept right on talking.

"I mean, I came in at six, and the TV's always on in the back office—it's not like I turned it on. Mr. Monroe keeps it on an all-news station all the time. So Cody Roberts saved both of you, didn't he? So that means he's a real-life action-adventure hero, right? Not just in the movies?"

Jen took this in, not knowing what to say. *Cody an actor? In movies?*

Now she got why he'd looked slightly familiar to her.

The girl behind the counter was leaning forward eagerly, so incredibly excited to be talking to her. She was practically hyperventilating, one question tumbling into the next.

"So you actually *saw* Cody Roberts up close and personal, right? Is he as good-looking in person as he is in the movies? Is he as tall as he looks? Is it really true that he does all his own stunts? I mean, the newscaster said that that whole video looks just like one of his action-adventure movies! I can't *wait* to see it!"

Jen stared down at the bill in her hands, unsure how to deal with these rapid-fire questions. She'd always been a very private person and had absolutely no idea how to handle this. And for one horrible moment she wondered if anyone knew about the night she'd spent with Cody. Anyone but the two of them.

Would she find herself on the cover of one of the tabloids? She didn't really know Cody at all. Would he tell the media about what they'd shared after the robbery? Sell a story for the money?

The minute she thought of the idea, she dismissed it. She wasn't a woman who made up stories in her head about men, no matter how much she cared for them. She had no desire to be a drama queen. And she'd always been a good judge of character.

Jen also trusted her own intuition, and it rarely failed her.

Ultimately she had always followed her heart, and it had gotten her in a lot of emotional trouble with what was left of her family. But it was as natural to her as breathing, and she wasn't about to stop now.

Cody hadn't told a soul. Intuitively she knew this the way she knew her own name. That time they'd spent together in her motel room had been as great a comfort to him as it had been to her. She'd sensed an honorable quality in him; he had those old-fashioned virtues so out of style in today's world.

He wasn't a man who would kiss and tell. If he could help it, his private life would remain private. And he was probably just as disturbed by this turn of events as she was.

"Are you all right?" The girl behind the counter had forgotten about her questions and now was worried about her. "Do you need to sit down? I could get you some water or make you some tea."

"No." Jen felt as if she were coming out of a fog. "No, I'm fine."

Reassured, the girl continued talking. "He's just such a hunk, you know? And I think he's a really good actor! Did you see him in *Deadly Prey?* He was just great in that. It's the one where he's this treasure hunter and he—"

Jen wanted to get away from all this, get out on the road, be anonymous for a while. She didn't want to remember the robbery. She wanted to reach Los Angeles this evening and start her new life.

"You're sure you're okay?" the girl asked, and Jen realized she'd been totally unresponsive, and that was probably what this woman thought was odd.

"Really sure. Thank you for caring." Jen looked down and saw that the printed bill was slightly crumpled in her hand. She eased her grip on the paper, then made herself smile at the young clerk. It wasn't her fault that she was caught up in a frenzy the media had created. She was at a gullible age, and this kind of craziness over a celebrity was so much a part of the current culture.

Looking at the eager, young freckled face, Jen said softly, "He's as wonderful as you think he is. And tall. And you can tell anyone you know who likes his movies that, as far as I'm concerned, Cody Roberts doesn't just play action heroes, he is one."

"I *knew* it!" the girl said jubilantly as Jen started out the lobby's glass door and into the bright desert sunshine.

THE GIRL BEHIND THE COUNTER at the motel wasn't the only one who had seen the video footage on the morning news.

Jen felt the glances directed at her as she drove through a fast-food outlet for a quick sandwich and the server who handed her her bag gave her a very strange look.

And Jen decided at that moment that she would have as little contact with the rest of the world as was humanly possible during the remainder of her drive.

Common sense told her that inevitably another story would take the place of the one currently leading in the news. Someone else would do something, something else would happen and she would be off the hook.

But until that time she would lay low.

JUST MY LUCK, CODY THOUGHT, *that today we shoot the love scene.*

Most action pictures had them, along with the paper-thin female role—the hero's generic girlfriend or wife. Or that classic staple, the hooker or bad girl with a heart of gold.

Movies rarely gave women good parts in action pictures; the focus was on the special effects, then the hero and his journey. What little was left was given to the female lead, if you could even call such a role a lead.

This picture's script was a little better written than most. It was one of the reasons Cody had auditioned for the role. At the height of his career, he'd cornered the market on tough, no-nonsense, alpha-male heroes with a cocky sense of humor, a quirky outlook on the world and rock-solid values.

Though the movies could have all had caricatures for the lead character and Cody could have easily played them that way, he'd worked with an acting coach. Cody had tried to make interesting choices, adding bits of humor and unexpected reactions and details to humanize his characters.

The actress playing the part of his wife in this movie was a friend of Cody's. They'd worked together before, and he knew her husband, Stan. He'd even spent one Thanksgiving with their family.

"Close your eyes and think of England," Carolyn joked as she sat on the edge of the bed on the set in a plush terry robe.

"Just pretend I'm Stan."

She laughed at that, and they got down to work.

"GREAT WORK," TREVOR COMMENTED when they finished the scene. "You're giving me great stuff, Cody."

Cody simply nodded. It hadn't been that hard. He'd been thinking of Jen the entire time, and the emotions had come to him simply and easily. He'd substituted Jen for Carolyn in his mind. He'd kissed Carolyn the way he wanted to kiss Jen, had touched the actress the way he wanted to touch Jen. She'd been in his mind and heart the entire time, and the scene had gone off without a hitch.

He wondered where she was. Somewhere on the road between Phoenix and Los Angeles, if her trip was going as planned. He wondered if she'd discovered that they were all over the news, that someone had found a celebrity in the midst of a robbery and thought it would make great entertainment.

And the moment the thought entered his head, he knew she would handle it. She might be small and curvy and blond, but there was a strength to Jen that would see her through this. If she could get through a robbery, she could get through the inconvenience of becoming—for hopefully a very short time—a public person.

And he would help her, once this shoot was done and he was back on the West Coast.

JEN HAD REACHED PALM SPRINGS, about two hours outside Los Angeles, when she decided she really had to pull over and get something besides fast food.

She didn't normally eat it, didn't care for it all that much. But the idea of not having to face more than two people—the cashier and the person who would hand her the bag of food—was tempting.

Now she needed some real food and some time outside her car. She also needed to fill up her gas tank, so she took one of the exits off the 10 West and headed into the famous desert town.

The first gas station had reasonable prices, so she pulled her car up to one of the pumps and cut the ignition.

And saw the dog.

A yellow Lab, a big, gangly puppy, the animal was all legs and paws and skinny ribs, with a madly whipping, wagging tail. Thin and desperately friendly, the pup was trying to climb into the open car door right across from her.

"Get the hell out of my car!" a large woman in a garishly flowered top and stretch polyester pants yelled. The animal cowered, darted back, then started toward another car.

The Lab puppy approached an old man who was pumping gas into his battered white truck. The dog slunk along on its belly, totally submissive, desperate to make a connection.

Jen couldn't take her eyes off the animal.

She ran into the small mini-mart and bought the best of what was available—a package of beef jerky. Once outside, she saw the puppy being shooed away from yet another car.

"Come here," she called, squatting down on the cement, in the shade, keeping her voice soft. She'd always loved animals, though her father had not allowed any while she'd been growing up. So she'd lavished love on her friends' cats and dogs and always thought of having a dog once she had her own home. It had been on her list of things to do, once she'd started her new life.

Funny how the universe gave you exactly what you needed at exactly the right time. She studied the puppy closely.

"Hey, girl," she called again, and the puppy saw her. Or more probably smelled the jerky. Jen had ripped open the packet and now held a piece of it in front of her.

Something about the way the puppy gamboled up to her, almost pushing her over in its eagerness to get something to eat, made her eyes sting. She gave the young Lab three pieces and made a friend for life.

As she went back to pump gas into her Mustang, the puppy never left her side. In fact, Jen felt her pressing her furry body against her legs, as the animal fairly quivered with excitement and reaction.

"It's okay now," she said, reaching down to pet the slightly grimy head. Her fur would be really soft once she'd had a bath.

"It's okay," she said again and realized she was saying it as much to herself as to her new dog.

6

One thing Cody had learned in all his years of being on movie sets was that you spent a lot of time waiting, especially for the lights to be set up. Therefore, you could choose to be bored and impatient or you could accept the wait and find something to do.

He usually came to work the first day with his lines down cold, fully memorized, overall and scene objectives thought about, his script totally marked up with the various choices he'd made. But he'd decided early on that he would choose not to be bored by all the waiting a movie actor did, all the time he found at his disposal. He'd find something to keep himself amused.

He'd never really been the kind of person who hid away in his trailer. He'd always talked with the crew, gotten to know everyone. When you were working this intensely with very talented people for a number of months, it made sense to make the process as painless as possible.

The only thing that had ever really prevented him from accomplishing this was the occasional director from hell or a costar who was a major pain in the ass.

But today, after Trevor had complimented him on

his work and started to set up for the next scene, Cody had decided he needed some privacy. So he'd headed for his trailer, and as soon as the door had shut behind him, he'd taken a deep breath and sat down in one of the comfortable chairs.

He couldn't stop thinking about Jen.

He wondered where she was, what she was doing, what she was thinking. He wondered what kind of a life she was running toward, because he could spot someone who was running away. It had felt as if she'd been on her last legs, that if this didn't work, she'd have nowhere to go, nowhere to hide.

It didn't feel as if she were afraid, as if there were a jealous or abusive husband in the picture. She hadn't been wearing any rings. But something about the whole thing still didn't sit right with him. A woman like Jen on the open road—she didn't seem like the sort of woman who was used to taking a road trip.

A candy-apple-red Mustang packed to the gills wasn't first-class travel accommodations.

He wondered what she'd heard about him. By now she certainly knew what he did for a living. If she were smart, she'd do a little research on him— and she might not like what she found.

If someone had told him when he was younger and working after school on the family ranch that he would become an actor, a bona fide international box-office star, he would have laughed in their faces.

But it had happened.

He'd been visiting his aunt Julianne and his cousin Keith in Los Angeles just after he turned twenty-one. His mother had insisted he needed a vacation, a change of scenery, and talked him into taking ten days to visit her sister and see something else of the country.

Everything he'd wanted at the time had been in Texas. He loved working with his father, loved the vast open skies of their small horse ranch outside of Austin.

But he'd humored his mother and agreed to see a little of the world.

He'd had dinner with his aunt and cousin at an Italian restaurant in Westwood, near the campus of UCLA, and afterward they had all been walking along Wilshire Boulevard on that autumn night when a woman had approached Cody.

"Are you an actor?" she'd asked him, breathless. Short, plump and very blond, dressed in black, she'd been gasping for breath, having run down the block after him.

"No."

"Would you like to be?"

"What?" The whole thing had seemed ludicrous.

"I could get you work in a heartbeat. You could make a lot of money. You look like—I mean, you look like a cowboy right off the ranch."

Probably because I am….

His aunt and cousin had watched in amusement as his Texas upbringing had prevented him from being anything but courteous to this woman and he'd finally accepted her business card. He'd tucked it into his wallet with the promise to call her first if he ever decided to go into the business.

It had been nothing but a chance encounter that

would make an amusing story to tell back home. Nothing more.

Until he'd gone back to Texas and discovered that his father was in debt up to his ears. A couple of bad business decisions had put the ranch in jeopardy, and his father was so prideful and stubborn that even Cody's mother didn't know how bad their financial situation was.

He was their only child and he knew what he had to do.

You could make a lot of money….

Though his father hadn't agreed with him, Cody had checked out the woman he'd met that night to make sure she was legitimate and discovered she worked for one of the biggest agencies in the entertainment industry. He'd called her long-distance, and she'd remembered him instantly. That had been all the incentive he'd needed.

He'd had to make a bold move to help his parents and he hadn't hesitated. He'd taken his savings and gone back out to L.A. He'd bunked at his aunt's house for the first six weeks, contacted the agent and she had been as good as her word.

He'd gotten a job within the week.

It had been a confusing time. Used to wide-open spaces and endless skies, he'd had to adapt to a concrete jungle, constant traffic and a cramped studio apartment. But he had and he'd worked and there had been something that had clicked. Just as his agent had predicted, audiences couldn't take their eyes off him in the small parts he played.

He'd had to do it all at once—learn the business,

take double and triple scene work in his acting classes to catch up with the men and women who had wanted to do this all their lives.

He'd felt like a fraud, but that was nothing compared to the relief he'd felt when he'd sent his father ridiculous amounts of money for work Cody had considered much less taxing than repairing fences and working the horses.

He'd even signed a contract to be the representative of a famous men's cologne, no matter how secretly ridiculous he'd felt that long afternoon in the photographer's studio "looking like a sexy cowboy." Money was money, and Cody was determined to help his parents.

Then his break had come.

A western, *The Survivor*, starring an Academy Award-winning actor known for his sheer, raw talent, came up. Cody knew he could play the part of the younger brother. He'd aced the audition, and the casting people had loved the fact that he looked great—and natural—in the saddle, could really lasso a steer and seemed to embody the part of the main character's little brother in a dramatic story set on a ranch in Montana.

The film had gone on to win all sorts of awards, and Cody had officially arrived. The part of the doomed, heroic younger brother who sacrificed his life for his family had seemed tailor-made for him.

He'd even been nominated for a Best Supporting Actor Oscar, and though he'd gotten all dressed up in a tux and attended the ceremonies with a female friend from his acting class, he hadn't won.

But his price had escalated, and now that his father was safely out of debt, the true irony occurred. He'd realized he really loved the actual process of acting. He found a new acting coach who'd opened up all sorts of worlds for him. And Cody discovered that he had a true passion for creating characters.

Those first few years had been good....

The knock on his trailer door startled him out of his thoughts.

"We'll be ready for you in about another hour, Cody."

"Thanks," he called back, then his thoughts returned to Jen.

He considered calling her. He had her cell number. Then, as soon as he thought of calling, he thought maybe it was too soon. Maybe she would consider him to be too pushy, too invasive.

Then Cody had to smile at the direction his thoughts were taking. Nothing about their entire relationship had been normal, even down to the way it had started.

He'd call her this evening. See how she was doing. Hell, he'd call her when they broke for dinner. Knowing Trevor, it would probably be a late dinner, but he'd make sure he had time to at least leave a message on her cell.

THE LAST PART OF THE DRIVE was going smoothly. The sun had set, and Jen thought there was something about driving a car at night, alone—except for her new dog—that was so soothing.

The scenery had changed once she'd left the Palm

Springs area, the desert giving way to low, rolling hills. She'd reconsidered the wisdom of sitting down in an actual restaurant once she'd picked up the dog, so they'd found an In-N-Out Burger drive-through on the outskirts of town. She'd laughed out loud at the comically grateful look on the stray's face when the pup had realized that a hot, freshly made and incredibly juicy hamburger was coming out of the takeout window, into the car and eventually into her stomach.

To a dog, a drive-through had to be a version of doggie heaven.

Jen petted her new canine friend.

Another bonus to having this dog as a traveling companion was that the animal was so cute, all attention was taken off her. By the time anyone finally looked at her and began to get that faint gleam of recognition in their eyes, she was already pulling out onto the open road and freedom.

"So you see," she'd said to the puppy as its tail wagged frantically, "you're already pulling your weight." The Lab looked beseechingly at the small carton of French fries, and Jen gave her one.

She wasn't worried about what her friend Maria was going to say about the puppy. Maria's mother bred prize-winning German shepherds, so Maria had never been without at least two dogs. She loved all animals and would fall in love with this yellow Lab as quickly as Jen herself had.

Now she had only about one hour of her road trip left, according to the signs on the road. Los Angeles was about fifty-four miles away. Even with traffic, she was going the opposite direction of rush hour, so it wouldn't be long before she arrived at Maria's doorstep.

A hot bath, a comfortable bed and the promise of total privacy from the outside world had never felt more appealing.

The puppy—Jen hadn't named her yet, feeling that the right name would present itself in the next few days—lay curled up on the passenger seat. Jen had spread a soft pink towel out on the upholstery and had also asked the woman at the drive-through for a few extra disposable drink cups so she could give the puppy water from her bottle in the backseat.

The puppy was behaving beautifully, in the way of strays so grateful for any kindness given to them.

When her cell rang, she picked it up. She'd been dreading answering it all day, as she knew her father would watch the news sooner or later. If that bit of video had made it to the Chicago area, she knew he would call and demand that she come home. He hadn't wanted her to take this trip in the first place.

But she checked caller ID, and the area code was Arizona's.

Cody.

"Hi."

"Hey, Jen. It's Cody."

Warmth and pleasure rushed through her at the sound of his voice. Happiness that he'd wanted to talk to her this soon, that he'd wanted to connect with her as much as she'd wanted to connect with him. Relief that it wasn't her father.

"Hey," she said back. "How are you?"

"Taking a dinner break. Thought I'd check and see how your trip's going."

"I'm about an hour outside of Los Angeles."

The puppy whined, then shifted her weight so her head rested in Jen's lap. She couldn't pet her, as one hand held the phone and the other was on the car's steering wheel. She always made a point of being an extra-attentive driver while on her cell.

"Do I hear whining?" Cody said.

"Not from me." Briefly she told him about the puppy.

"That's one lucky dog. Strays don't do too well in the desert heat."

"Tell me about it."

"How old is she?" he said.

"I'd guess about four or five months."

"Just the right age to be dumped when a puppy's no longer cute."

"Exactly," Jen said. "I'm so glad I found her. It broke my heart the way she was trying to get into everyone's car at the gas station."

"So you have a habit of picking up strays."

She heard beyond the words to what he was really saying.

"You," she said softly, "are no stray." She sighed, knowing there was no place for anything but honesty in the relationship they were building. "I finally figured out where I've seen you before. You're an action-adventure actor, right?"

"I stand accused."

She laughed. "So that's why the security tape made the news."

He laughed, and she liked the sound of it. "Don't believe anything you see about a celebrity on television. The stuff they make up is a lot more entertaining than the truth. Most of the time."

There was a short silence—but it wasn't uncomfortable—before Cody said, "You having any trouble with being notorious?"

"I've gotten a few looks, but I've kept to the road and limited my time with people to a few drive-throughs and gas stations. Most of the women just want to know about you."

"Yeah, yeah, yeah."

She could sense he was embarrassed about the attention and said, "It doesn't bother me."

"Want some advice?"

"I'd love some."

"Get to your friend's house as soon as you can. Make sure no one follows you. Stay low for a few days, until something else makes the news and this whole thing blows over."

"That sounds good."

"What about the kid?" Cody said, and Jen was suddenly fiercely glad that her first impression of this man had been correct. He had a great and generous heart and was able to think of people other than himself. He remembered the young cashier, Johnny.

Quite a few actors would have been incapable of seeing this incident in any other way except how it affected their career. She was so thankful that Cody could see beyond the superficial, to other people and how their lives were touched.

A lot of people, in her experience, couldn't seem to make that leap.

"I'm going to call his mom tonight or early tomorrow and see how he's doing."

"You got his home number? Why am I not surprised."

She told him about Johnny and his mother, a little about what had happened once the police had arrived at the scene.

"He's so lucky to have a mom like that," she said.

"You don't have a mother," he said, and she realized she was getting used to his perceptive approach and the emotionally direct questions.

"No."

"Neither do I. Something else we have in common."

She heard a noise in the background, then Cody said, "I have to go. I'll call you tomorrow night, okay?"

"I'd like that," she said and hung up her phone. Sliding it back into her purse, she put her free hand on the puppy's head, gently stroking the grimy ears.

She couldn't stop smiling.

JUST TALKING TO HER PUT HIM in a better mood.

It wasn't as if he'd been looking for a relationship when he'd found Jen. An actual relationship with a woman he could be intimate with had been much further down the list of things he wanted to get done.

Number one had been to do some work on himself, to climb out of the hole he'd dug for himself.

He'd helped his father get out of debt, but he hadn't counted on his dying soon after. A ranching accident, nothing anyone could have predicted. But it had shattered both his and his mother's world completely, and he hadn't been able to get out of the downward spiral his life had become. Until now.

On the road to where he someday wanted to be, his first priority had been to get his life in order. Finish this particular movie. Prove that he was a dependable actor, able to complete a picture. He didn't even want to think beyond to how the movie might do at the box office, even though the press had already labeled it his comeback.

And he couldn't think about how the powers that be might spin the robbery to their advantage.

But Jen… She'd been a complete surprise. The time he'd spent with her in her motel room had opened him up. Made him feel again. He'd spent so much time shut down, doing anything to prevent feeling and then found this woman who made it so effortless to do just that.

She might have come at the completely wrong time. He might not be ready for her. But he was going to keep in touch with her, call her on a regular basis, get to know her.

And when he got back to Los Angeles, he was going to see her. Because Cody trusted his intuition, and everything was telling him not to let this woman drift out of his life.

SHE'D ARRIVED AT MARIA'S house a little after eight-thirty that same evening. The drive shouldn't have taken so long, but with rest stops for the dog and the time she'd taken to get out and walk once in a while in secluded spots, time had just gotten away from her.

She'd called Maria when she'd been about a mile from her house and prepped her for the dog.

"Poor thing! We'll give her a bath and some food and she'll feel much better." Jen had smiled. She could picture her friend, with her shiny dark brown hair pulled up in a haphazard twist, her brown eyes soft and warm, her personality one of utter generosity.

A bath. Maria was nothing if not practical. She was one of those people who knew what had to be done and got down to it.

Her friend would never have been able to afford a house in Los Angeles; real estate there was incredibly expensive. But her mother had bought a house just off Melrose Avenue decades ago, a rental, and had given it to Maria for as long as she needed it, along with a substantial loan to make a success of her coffeehouse.

And shortly after she pulled her car around back of Maria's spacious stucco, Spanish-style house, with its cream walls and red tile roof, the puppy was getting her bath in one of Maria's bathrooms. The Lab puppy was up to her ears in suds, while Maria's two German shepherds, Kaya and Sheba, and her Yorkshire terrier, Gizmo, watched anxiously from the tiled floor.

"You'd think they were getting the bath," Maria said, laughing as the puppy wriggled under their grasp, then shook and sprayed soapy, citrus-scented bubbles on both of them.

"They're good dogs, they didn't even mind her," Jen said. She stayed at the puppy's head, offering more reassurance than actual washing. But Maria was all business as she cleaned the stray. She'd helped her mother get her dogs ready for shows for years, so she had the whole routine down pat.

Within fifteen minutes the puppy was standing on a thick towel and being dried by two others. Her tail wagged so hard, her entire backside wiggled.

"She's a happy girl," Maria said. "We can take her to my vet tomorrow."

"That would be great."

"Think we can get there without starting a riot?" Maria said, giving her a sly sideways glance.

"Oh God, you saw the news, too?"

"Who didn't? I wasn't sure what was going on, so I haven't told anyone that the woman who was at that robbery was you."

"Thanks. I think I'd just like to hide out here for a few days."

"Are you okay, Jen?"

The simple, caring question caught her off guard. Maria had hugged her hard when she'd pulled into her driveway and stepped out of her car. Then they'd talked and talked while they'd unloaded everything, pulled the car in back of the house and gave the puppy water and food.

This had been the first moment they'd been able to really discuss what had happened.

"Better than I should be," she said slowly, carefully choosing her words. "I think it's because of Cody."

"What's he like?"

Trust Maria to not believe all the media and hype.

"Wonderful. He was— We talked and he—he helped me through the whole thing."

"I thought he left right after the whole thing went down."

"He caught up with me on the road." That wasn't too big a white lie, but she wasn't ready to tell even her closest friend the intimate details of what had really happened.

"He always seemed like a really great guy. I never understood what happened, why his career was so derailed."

"What happened?" Jen asked, unable to avoid the puppy's pink tongue and her grateful wet kisses. Not really wanting to.

"I guess it all happened after his father died. Some kind of accident on their ranch in Texas. Cody left the business to help out at home, but it all went downhill from there. The news was never really clear about what happened. I got the impression he's kind of a private guy—about his real life, I mean. Off the screen."

"Hmm," was all she said in return.

"But, man, that video. I was working, the television was on behind the counter and I almost dropped two double lattes when I saw you."

"It was pretty bad," Jen said, then hugged the puppy to her, wet-dog smell and all. This was the life she'd thought was over while down on that floor. This was what she'd never thought she'd have again—just a simple talk with a close friend.

"Does your father know?"

"If he's watched the news, he does. He also has my cell number."

"And he hasn't called you yet?" Maria arched a

delicate, dark brow. "Oh, baby, he's marshaling his forces. He's getting his arguments ready as to why you should come straight home—now! He's probably got your plane ticket all locked and loaded."

"No," was all Jen said.

"You're welcome to stay here as long as you want—you know that."

"I do." Jen reached for her friend's hand, grabbed it, squeezed it. "And you don't know what that means to me."

"Hey, I want you to have the life you want. And who else can bake the best chocolate-chip cookies to go with a cup of coffee since Mrs. Fields? I'm going to make you earn your keep."

Jen had to laugh at that. She knew Maria was joking, that she could bake cookies or not, do whatever she wanted while she stayed with her in Los Angeles. Maria only wanted what was best for her and had since they'd met in college in a creative-writing class. They'd simply clicked and had kept journals from that day forward and had shared the dreams they'd written down with each other.

Jen was taking the wet towels and putting them in the washing machine just off the kitchen, the puppy dancing at her heels, when she heard her cell ring.

And knew it could only be one person.

7

"JENNIFER, I'VE ALREADY BOUGHT your ticket. Of course you're coming home."

Jen shut her eyes as she leaned against her closed bedroom door. Maria had taken all the dogs outside, and Jen knew if she walked to the window and looked down, she'd see them all playing in the dark yard, the only illumination the lights surrounding the back patio. At this exact moment she wished she was down there with them.

"Dad," she said, then took a deep breath.

He didn't give her the chance to get the words out of her mouth. Randolph Whitney hadn't reached lofty heights in the world of business by being a pushover.

"I saw the video on the news, Jennifer. It's time for you to come home."

She sighed, rubbing the tight furrow between her brows, trying to ease the tension. Most of the time when she talked with her father, she got a headache afterward. But she was stubborn, as she knew she had to be when dealing with him, and she refused to simply give up on the relationship between them.

He was the only close blood relative she had left.

For so many years, having a close relationship with her father, even though he could be so unfeeling, had been one of the top priorities in her life.

She could picture him now, sitting in the leather chair in his comfortable den, phone at hand, the frown on his face causing his forehead to wrinkle. Though his dark hair was frosted with gray, he still had the vigor and physique of a much younger man.

The one thing about her father that frustrated her immensely was that he could only see one viewpoint ever—his own.

"I can't come back, Dad."

"Can't or *won't?*" Her father's voice sounded tense. Cold. If it had been a visible thing, she envisioned it as a sword, sharp and deadly. Cutting. She knew he wanted what he thought was best for her, for his sense of who she was and what she could be.

The only problem was, his idea of the life she should lead had nothing to do with who she really was. Long ago she'd given up trying to make him understand.

"Won't," she said quietly. And with what she hoped was finality.

"I cannot approve of this," he said. "I'm going to give you the flight information, and I want you home. I've bought you a one way ticket. Jennifer, you belong in Chicago. You belong with Ethan, even though you don't choose to see it that way. You know I'm right."

"Dad." Jen fought to keep her voice calm. She'd managed to stop seeking her father's approval, but there was still a little bit of an emotional sting. She wondered if there always would be. "Dad, I know you must have been scared to see what was on the news—"

"*Scared* doesn't even begin to cover what I felt."

"It was horrible. But it happened and it's over." Long ago she'd realized her father was one of those people who could only see events in life as they affected him, from his point of view. He couldn't seem to put himself in another person's place and think of how they might feel. She knew he wouldn't ask how she was or how she'd felt during those horribly long, frightening moments in the convenience store.

"And you were all over the national news with that...*actor.*"

She had to smile. Her father's innate snobbery knew no limits. If someone wasn't in his circle of acquaintances, then they just didn't count.

For him, actors registered somewhere way off that particular scale, probably level with the people who ran carnivals. For a moment she thought about what might happen if Cody and her father ever met. She couldn't even imagine it.

Her sense of mischief took over.

"They must have blurred my upper body if they showed the whole thing in prime time," she said.

"I simply cannot believe you're treating this whole incident as if it were some kind of joke."

"Sometimes, Dad," Jen said, choosing her words carefully, "that's the only way you can get through it."

"Have you seen the footage of the robbery yet? Have you even watched the news?"

"I'm not sure I want to," she said. She hadn't thought about it, but her gut told her that the last thing she wanted to do was relive the events of yesterday morning.

Silence. She was used to these silences with her father. He used long silences to intimidate, but those silences no longer intimidated her.

"All right. But enough is enough. Jennifer, you have to come home now. You've made your point—you drove across the country by yourself and reached Maria's house—but now you have to come home. It's not going to work out for you there when your home is back here."

"Does Ethan miss me?" she said, deliberately changing the subject.

"Of course he does. He was telling me how much just the other day."

She had to smile, a wry little grimace. Ethan would tell her father, yet he'd made no move to phone her, to discuss his feelings, to try and work things out. He'd simply looked at her like a stunned fish, his mouth open, when she'd given him back the expensive engagement ring at their last dinner together.

Ethan wasn't in the habit of not getting his way. He'd seemed flabbergasted at the thought that she didn't want to marry him. Like her father, he believed life worked in an orderly way, and emotions or feelings of any sort were to be avoided if at all possible.

He hadn't come to see her after that. Instead, she guessed, he'd asked her father out for a drink, and the two of them had discussed her and how to "handle things."

How to handle her. How to do what was best for her, which translated into doing what was best for them. Neither of them had ever had a clue as to what she needed or wanted. Though she loved her father deeply and had spent many years trying to help him to understand what she needed, Ethan was a different matter.

Ethan was just Ethan. Totally safe. Very financially secure and entirely without passion. Her father had selected him for her, and her life would have continued along the same path she'd lived with him, simply switching one man for the other, but the emotional feel of their life would be the same. Making a home with him, never running too quickly or laughing too loudly. Simply being the bird in the cage, beating her wings against the bars.

"Jennifer? Are you coming home?"

"I'm thinking." And she was.

After college, her father had created a job for her within his company—really nothing more than a glorified executive secretary. She hadn't wanted it, but he had made her promise she would at least try it for one year. The routine had become habit, and she'd spent almost three years there—three quietly unhappy years—wondering what she was going to do with her life.

Later she'd realized he'd created this job to keep her within his control until he found the perfect man for her—Ethan. Then her job would be to go home and be the perfect business wife and mother. Not to bother either her father or Ethan or intrude in any way. She and her children would remain at home. They would behave.

The thought of her children having the same childhood she'd endured was enough to make her scream. When she'd visited Maria in Los Angeles and learned she was opening a coffeehouse, every dream Jen had

ever had had come to the surface and fought to get
out with a vengeance.

And it had been on the day following Maria's an-
nouncement, after Jen had spent the night in bed
with stomach cramps and a headache, that she had
finally realized that she wanted a life that was hers.
She wanted to create a life she loved. Talking to
Maria, her plan had been born.

"Ethan misses you terribly," her father said.

Jen didn't reply. As badly as she wanted a life of
her own, she knew she might have turned back if it
hadn't been for the robbery. How strange, but now
she looked on it as a blessing in disguise.

If not for those few hours in Cody's arms and the
experience that had shown her there was a whole different way to be intimate with a man, she might have
been tempted to go back to her safe life, to her father's and then her husband's care. But she wasn't
going back to her safe life. She couldn't, not after
today. Not now and not ever.

All of these thoughts flashed through her mind
within seconds before she replied to what her father
had said.

"No," she said.

"No, Ethan doesn't miss you? What are you talking about, Jennifer? Try to make some sense, I'm having trouble following you."

"No, I'm not coming home," she said, keeping her
voice steady and low. "I love you very much, Dad,
but I'm staying out here. It will all blow over."

"Love has nothing to do with it. I want you to
come home. You have to come home. Today."

He was so used to getting his own way.

"No," she said again. "No, Dad, I can't come home. I'll call you later in the week, but I need to go now. I love you."

And with that she gently disconnected their call, knowing he wouldn't call back. Not right away. Not until he'd thought their call through, marshaled his ideas, formulated his plan and decided how to get around her decision once and for all.

"I'M PROUD OF YOU," MARIA SAID. She'd ordered in a pizza, and now they sat, just after eleven o'clock, in her comfortable living room, the dogs around them. Maria had built the large adobe fireplace by herself, and tonight it was filled with white candles of varied heights, their flickering glow casting the entire room in a soft light.

"Thanks," Jen said, reaching for her glass of wine.

"It has to be hard dealing with him."

"You get used to it." Jen reached down and scratched the puppy's ears. Her fur was just as soft as she'd known it would be after the bath.

"You need a name for this little girl," Maria said.

"It'll come to me."

"Take it easy tomorrow," Maria said, and Jen could tell that her friend was going into her planning mode. It was something that served her quite well in her business.

"Sleep in as late as you like, then take a long bath. I'll leave you some of Cody's DVDs in the den, and you can watch him to your heart's content. Just take a lazy day. It's not like you don't deserve one after what you've been through."

"It's almost like—" Jen hesitated, then continued. "It's like I can't quite process it. Like it happened to someone else. One moment I'm fine, then something triggers a memory and I feel all—"

"Scared?"

"Yeah. And shaky."

"Nothing bad's going to happen here. I have a great alarm system, and burglars just hate my dogs. If Kaya and Sheba don't look like they'd eat them and that fails to frighten them, the little yapper here draws too much attention to the break-in."

Jen started to laugh at the thought of Maria's ten-pound Yorkshire terrier, Gizmo, going up against anything or anyone. "I saw a show once about home robberies, and the ex-burglar said they hate little dogs the most because they're so noisy."

Maria grinned. "See? There's a method to my madness, with two large and one teeny one. Oh—I can bring a dog crate into your bedroom for your puppy, or he can just sleep on your bed with you. Whatever you want."

"I think I'd like the company," Jen admitted.

"Fine with me. The house is dogproof." Maria got up to go into the kitchen, and Jen noticed both her large shepherds stood with her, always by her side. Her Yorkie dozed in front of the fireplace, content.

"Jen?"

"Yeah?"

"You know where my bedroom is. I don't care what time it is or what it's about, if you need me or just need to talk, wake me up. Okay?"

Having come from a family that did not value emotions, and being an extremely emotional person herself, Maria's generosity overwhelmed Jen. Feeling rushed through her. Her eyes stung as they began to fill.

"Now look what you made me do," she said, teasing.

"I mean it," Maria said. "I've never been part of a robbery, but I can't imagine it was much fun."

SHE COULDN'T SLEEP.

Not surprising, the day she'd had. It felt like more than one day. An endless day. The drive, finding the puppy, then Maria's house, the dog bath, her father's call, a late dinner and now lying in bed trying to settle down and sleep.

Something her canine friend had no trouble with. The puppy was sprawled out across the queen-size bed, snuggled up against her, so grateful for her new, warm home, her full stomach and just simple caring.

She heard her cell ring and—as she'd placed it by the bedside table—she found it easily. It was almost midnight in Los Angeles, two in the morning in Chicago, so she was sure it wasn't her father.

The number showed an Arizona area code, and her heart sped up.

"Hello?" she said, and her voice sounded tentative to her own ears.

"Am I calling too late?"

"No," she said.

"Are you having as much trouble sleeping as I am?"

"Yes." The one word came out on a sigh.

"What happens when you close your eyes?"

He knew. He knew what she was going through.

"I still see the whole thing all over again," she admitted. "Different parts, but it's…frightening."

"Me, too."

"How do you get past it?" she said.

"I don't know. Time would be my guess, but that doesn't help us now. I think the first few nights will probably be the most difficult."

"I wish you were here with me," she said, then stopped, astonished at the words that had come out of her mouth so easily. She wasn't used to asking for things.

"I wish I could be there."

"I didn't mean that the way it might have sounded—"

"I know what you meant. Just to be next to someone who understands what you're going through."

A short silence, totally comfortable, then Jen said, "I felt so safe when I slept with you. I'm not sure why. You just have that feeling about you."

"Thanks. It was good for me, too. The sleeping, I mean." He paused. "Actually everything with you was good. Is good. Am I making sense?"

"Yes."

"That's good."

"What is?"

"I hear a smile in your voice."

She couldn't stop smiling. With any other man she would have thought it was too soon for him to call, too soon for them to talk on this level. One of her girlfriends had once told her about the thirty-six-hour rule when you met a man. If he called you within twenty-four hours, it was too soon and he was too needy. If he called you later than thirty-six hours, he wasn't all that interested.

But with Cody things had been different from the start. None of those rules applied to them.

"What are you doing?" she said.

"Lying in bed, trying to sleep, not succeeding, knowing I have to be up at five."

"Are you making a movie?"

She could feel his hesitation over the phone.

"I haven't seen all your movies, Cody, and I didn't connect you with them when we first met. I'd kind of—I'd like to keep it that way for now, if it's okay with you. But I'd like to see them all eventually."

"I know what you mean, Jen. I'd like that," he said. "I've kind of been off track with my career lately, so there wouldn't have been anything out for you to see."

"Do you feel like things are falling back into place for you?"

"Now they are."

She didn't want to read too much into what he was saying, so for now she didn't.

"How's the pooch?" he said.

"On the bed with me. Maria and I gave her a bath. She loved her dinner, and tomorrow she's going to the vet's."

"I'm sure she'll enjoy that. What've you decided to name her?"

"I don't know. It'll come to me. Names always do."

"I know what you mean."

"Do you have any animals?"

He laughed. "Ten horses, a burro, two rescued potbellied pigs, three dogs and two cats."

"And you have a one-bedroom apartment?" she said, teasing him.

"A small ranch. Just outside Santa Barbara."

"It sounds beautiful."

"It is. It's like my...sanctuary. You'll have to come see it when I get back."

"I'd love to." She glanced at her bedside clock. "You have to get up in a few hours."

"Yeah, I know. And you have to get some sleep. I just thought I'd check in. Feel any better?"

"Much. You?"

"Yeah, I do. You have sweet dreams, Jenny. I'll give you a call in the next few days." He laughed. "Probably tomorrow."

She laughed, as well, then they said their good-byes and hung up. And when she rolled over and plumped her pillow, Jen smiled and realized she wasn't as afraid anymore.

When she closed her eyes, she didn't see the inside of a convenience store or the barrel of a sawed-off shotgun. Instead she saw rolling hills and a ranch, pot-bellied pigs and a burro.

Exhausted, she finally slept.

ONE THING JENNIFER HAD ALWAYS known about herself was that she was the sort of person who liked to stay busy. So, very early in the morning, after she pulled on her robe and slippers and went down to the kitchen just before Maria left to go to work, she asked her friend what needed to be done around the house.

"Nope. Nothing. Stop that, Jen, I want you to take a day off. I mean it!"

"Come on, you know me, I'll go crazy if there's nothing to do!" Jen reached down and patted the puppy's head. The yellow Lab followed her everywhere she went, not wanting to let her out of its sight.

Maria considered what she'd said as she shrugged into her lightweight jacket. "Okay. Do you still like to mess around in the garden and do things with plants?"

"Love it."

"I have a bunch of houseplants on the back porch that need to be repotted. The soil and the pots are right next to them because I've been planning to get to them for the last few weeks and just haven't."

"Great. That, I can do. And I'll make some cookies for the coffeehouse."

"Fine. Just don't get too ambitious. Leave yourself some downtime, okay? And remember, we're taking what's-her-name to the vet's late this afternoon, so you have to think up a name for the poor thing."

Jen agreed, but what she didn't tell her friend was that she wanted to exhaust herself, to wear herself out so she could sleep through the night and not dream about being back inside that convenience store in the middle of a robbery.

Once Maria left, Jen showered and dressed, then let the four dogs out into the backyard and, armed with a cup of coffee, decided to take on the plants.

The disorder that confronted her made her laugh. Maria might be a genius at her business, but there were still a few things around her house that stumped her. Plants were one of those things.

"A black thumb," she'd said more than once. "That's what I have."

Easily twenty-five to thirty houseplants, in various bedraggled states, were grouped on the far end of the cement porch, just under the awning. A jumbo-sized sack of organic potting soil was propped against the side of the house, along with stacks of terra-cotta pots.

She glanced over, sipping her coffee, and saw that Gizmo was leading the two bigger dogs on a merry chase. It had always astounded Jen how the littlest dog ruled this particular roost.

But her Lab, her little golden girl, was right by her side, gazing up at her with adoring brown eyes. The dog's expression was still tinged with a sense of fear, as if she couldn't believe her luck and was just waiting for everything to disappear. In the meantime she'd stay close.

Just like a shadow, Jen thought.

Shadow.

She knelt down. "Shadow? Would you like that for your new name?"

The puppy wiggled and wagged, snuggled closer, licked her face, so Jen laughed and petted her. When Shadow rolled over on her back, she gave her a tummy rub.

"Shadow it is, and just in time for your trip to the vet!"

The puppy stayed right next to her as Jen sat down by the ailing houseplants and reached for the first one.

BY THE TIME MARIA GOT HOME at three, Jen had repotted all the houseplants and positioned them around the house and by the sliding glass door in back according to their need for light. She'd also hosed the dirt she'd spilled off the cement porch, done the breakfast dishes, played with the dogs, baked two dozen chocolate-chip cookies and cleaned up the kitchen from her baking spree.

The entire house smelled of chocolate, sugar and vanilla.

"Oh, honey, I'm home!" Maria called as she walked inside. The dogs had already started up a racket when they'd heard her car, and now she walked into complete canine pandemonium. "Oh my God, that smell! Where's my cookie?"

Jen laughed and handed her one. Then she had to laugh again at the expression of total ecstasy as Maria bit into the cookie, chewed, then swallowed.

"These are even better than I remember from last time! The compliments I got at my opening! People raved! Jen, you could make a living selling these."

"I don't think so."

"I *do* think so! What if I asked you for a standing order—say, five or six dozen a day?"

"I'd say you'd need a commercial kitchen."

"And what do you think I've been doing with the guesthouse?"

"You're kidding!"

"Nope. Right this way."

Maria's house had a guesthouse completely detached from the main house. As Jen followed her inside, she realized that Maria had remodeled the small house so that it qualified as a commercial kitchen.

"I'm not kidding, Jen. I can sell these cookies. I was going to hire someone else to do some baking for me until you asked if you could come out and stay here. Would you want to make them?"

She couldn't refuse her friend. And the idea of doing something slightly more creative than waiting on tables appealed to her. Maybe this was the life she was looking for, or at least one of the major forks in the road that she wanted to take.

"Yes. But I don't want anything to come between our friendship if this doesn't work out."

"Oh, please! As if that was ever a possibility—" Maria stopped as they walked back toward the house, just now noticing that the huge pile of ailing houseplants was no longer there. In its place, the larger plants—palms and climbing jasmine—surrounded the sliding glass door leading into the living room.

And overhead there were several hanging plants, now in bigger pots and combined in different ways. Jen had taken two or three of the more pathetic stragglers, pinched or cut them back and put them all in one hanging pot, creating a feeling of lushness.

"I can't believe these are the same plants! It looks like a greenhouse out here! What did you do?"

"Just combined a few to make one big plant, pinched some back, cut back a few others—"

"Okay, I want you to make those cookies, but I also want you to help me supply the coffeehouse with plants—and could you help me take care of them? I think—no, I *know*—I have a black thumb."

Jen had to laugh. Her friend was so transparent.

"You don't have to do this, Maria."

"What do you mean? I can't bake, I kill plants,

just about the only skill I have is that I make a mean cup of coffee and I love to talk to people. Come on, Jen, say yes! I've been thinking about this ever since you came out in January, and when you said you were moving, I knew this would work out."

"You're serious."

"You bet."

Jen hesitated, considering her friend's offer. She and Maria had always been close and she didn't think this would affect their friendship. And it felt right.

"Cookies and plants."

"Great cookies, *incredible* cookies, to go along with my exceptional coffee, and plants to help create the ambience I want."

"You're not just helping me out—"

"Hey, you'd be helping *me* out. I want to make A Bit of a Buzz into one of the major coffeehouses in this town! I'm even thinking of bringing in some music a few nights a week, maybe a poetry night, writers reading their work, all sorts of things. Jen, I need your help to make it a success!"

She could feel her throat closing, her eyes stinging. Everything seemed to hit her in a very emotional way since the robbery; it was as if her emotions were totally out of control. But it felt so good to know that Maria needed her.

Her father and Ethan hadn't needed her for anything. They'd just wanted her to stand on the sidelines and look beautiful, to be there when they needed her, to become the ultimate accessory.

It had never been about her doing anything. And that was what she'd come out west to find.

And Jen found that she wanted to help her friend. Maria had put her entire life on hold when her mother had been diagnosed with breast cancer. None of her other siblings had made the time, but Maria had been housekeeper, cook, medical advocate, masseuse and general cheerleader and kept her mother from sinking into despair for almost two years.

Though her friend had wanted nothing for what she'd done, her mother had given her this house, along with a loan to start up the coffeehouse of her dreams. It had caused a little bit of resentment with her siblings, but Maria had merely forged ahead.

Jen knew how long Maria had put her own dreams on hold and now Jen found she wanted to be a part of her friend's dream and, in doing so, make a few of her own come true.

"Yes," Jen said.

"You'll do it?"

"Yes."

"All right! Let's break out a bottle of—wait, we have to get what's-her-name to the vet's."

"Shadow."

"Shadow?"

"As in, me and my."

Jen watched as Maria considered the gangly Lab puppy practically glued to her side.

"Yep. Works for me. Let me get these guys in their crates and we'll take off."

They were backing out of the driveway, Shadow in another crate and Jen's hand at the crate's door, reassuring her, when Maria turned to her and said, "This is going to be great, Jen. I can feel it."

"I know."

She couldn't wait to tell Cody.

HE CALLED THAT NIGHT, RIGHT after dinner.

"Cookies, huh? That sounds like a lot of fun."

"It is. It never gets boring because I'm always on the lookout for new ways of doing things."

"Just don't mess with the classics," he warned her, and she laughed. Men.

"Okay. Are you a nuts-with-your-chocolate-chip-cookie or a purist?"

"A purist."

"Me, too." A sudden thought struck her. "Hey, do you have an address out there?"

"I do."

"Care to give it to me?"

He did.

"Now you have to tell me what this is all about," Cody said.

"Oh, I don't know, you just might find yourself receiving a little care package in the next few days."

"Cookies?"

The naked, blatant, masculine hope in his voice made her laugh out loud.

"I think that can be arranged."

She liked their time on the phone together. They shared their days, their feelings. The calls rarely ran longer than fifteen or twenty minutes; just enough to touch base and share their lives.

"I called Johnny's mother, Laura, today," Cody said.

Jen was touched. Cody had asked her for the number during one of their earlier calls. Now she felt guilty because she hadn't remembered to call and check up on Johnny.

"I completely forgot."

"Don't worry. She told me to send you her love."

"How are they doing? The whole family?"

"It's strange," Cody said. "After I introduced myself and we talked for a little bit, I asked her how things were. She said she and her husband and daughter were trying to be strong for Johnny. Then I asked how he was doing. She got really quiet, then said he was fine. She and her husband have arranged for him to see a therapist."

"That's probably wise."

"I asked her if she knew if this person had ever dealt with Critical Incident Stress before."

"You mean like those questions you asked me?"

"Yeah."

"What did she say?"

"She kind of shut off. I think the whole thing's been pretty overwhelming for her, as well. I didn't want to push things. I want to keep that connection open, you know?"

"Yeah, I do," Jen said, then yawned. "I'll make sure to call her tomorrow and I'll check up on what's up with Johnny."

"You're getting sleepy," he said. "I hope it's not the company."

"Never."

"I'll let you go," Cody said. "I'm glad Shadow got a clean bill of health from the vet, and I have a feeling you're going to get a good night's sleep because of all the work you did."

"I think so, too."

"Same grueling schedule tomorrow?"

"Tomorrow," Jen said, unable to keep the smile out of her voice, "I start my career as a cookie entrepreneur!"

"Congratulations, Jen. I'm happy for you."

8

JENNIFER SLEPT THROUGH THE night, but before waking the following morning, the images started. She was back in the convenience store, on the floor, and the man with the long, greasy black hair had his shotgun pointed right at her. She was fumbling with the clasp of her bracelet and couldn't seem to get it off. He was shouting, and she had the overwhelming sense that no one was going to help her. She was going to die—

Jen came awake with a start to find Shadow pressed up against her, a worried look on her furry face. One of her paws, the nails newly cut by the vet tech, was firmly on her chest; she could feel the pressure. The Lab puppy looked as if she were about to bark.

"Shhh," Jen said and placed a comforting hand on the puppy's soft head. "It's all right."

Shadow whined softly and removed her paw. Jen sighed. Her dog knew she wasn't speaking the truth. Nothing was fine as long as she kept having these horrific images in her mind.

She glanced at the bedside clock's illuminated face. A few minutes before six. Maria would already be at work; she opened her coffeehouse when the

An Important Message from the Editors

Dear Reader,

If you'd enjoy reading romance novels with larger print that's easier on your eyes, let us send you TWO FREE HARLEQUIN INTRIGUE® NOVELS in our NEW LARGER-PRINT EDITION. These books are complete and unabridged, but the type is set about 25% bigger to make it easier to read. Look inside for an actual-size sample.

By the way, you'll also get a surprise gift with your two free books!

Pam Powers

Peel off Seal and Place Inside...

LARGER-PRINT
FREE BOOKS
EDITION

84

THE RIGHT WOMAN

she'd thought she was fine. It took Daniel's words and Brooke's question to make her realize she was far from a full recovery.

She'd made a start with her sister's help and she intended to go forward now. Sarah felt as if she'd been living in a darkened room and someone had suddenly opened a door, letting in the fresh air and sunshine. She could feel its warmth slowly seeping into the coldest part of her. The feeling was liberating. She realized it was only a small step and she had a long way to go, but she was ready to face life again with Serena and her family behind her.

All too soon, they were saying goodbye and arah experienced a moment of sadness for all e years she and Serena had missed. But they d each other now and that's what

She held

PRINTED IN THE U.S.A.
Publisher acknowledges the copyright holder of the excerpt from this individual work as follows:
THE RIGHT WOMAN Copyright © 2004 by Linda Warren. All rights reserved.
® and TM are trademarks owned and used by the trademark owner and/or its licensee.

The Harlequin Reader Service™ — Here's How It Works:

Accepting your 2 free Harlequin Intrigue® larger-print books and gift places you under no obligation to buy anything. You may keep the books and gift and return the shipping statement marked "cancel." If you do not cancel, about a month later we'll send you 6 additional Harlequin Intrigue larger-print books and bill you just $4.49 each in the U.S., or $5.24 each in Canada, plus 25¢ shipping & handling per book and applicable taxes if any.* That's the complete price and — compared to cover prices of $5.24 each in the U.S. and $6.24 each in Canada — it's quite a bargain! You may cancel at any time, but if you choose to continue, every month we'll send you 6 more books, which you may either purchase at the discount price or return to us and cancel your subscription.

*Terms and prices subject to change without notice. Sales tax applicable in N.Y. Canadian residents will be charged applicable provincial taxes and GST.

If offer card is missing write to: Harlequin Reader Service, 3010 Walden Ave., P.O. Box 1867, Buffalo, NY 14240-1867

BUSINESS REPLY MAIL
FIRST-CLASS MAIL   PERMIT NO. 717-003   BUFFALO, NY

POSTAGE WILL BE PAID BY ADDRESSEE

HARLEQUIN READER SERVICE
3010 WALDEN AVE
PO BOX 1867
BUFFALO NY 14240-9952

NO POSTAGE
NECESSARY
IF MAILED
IN THE
UNITED STATES

sun rose in order to catch early-bird customers who needed their caffeine fix before work.

She was alone in the house. Alone with those images, alone with that horrible sense of—

Fear.

She lay back down among the covers and held on to Shadow, wondering if she would ever feel totally safe again. And, glancing at the clock one more time, saw her cell on the nightstand.

She thought of Cody.

He was probably already on the set. Busy. He wouldn't want to be bothered.

Yes, he would, a quiet little voice inside her said.

Damn it. She knew Cody would want to hear from her if she was scared. She was just afraid to call him. She didn't need years of therapy to know that, from what had happened with her father, she didn't have a whole lot of faith in men being there for her.

Do it, that little voice said: *Call him. Let him know you need him.*

Her hand shook as she reached for the phone.

CODY WAS EATING BREAKFAST with some of the crew when his cell rang. When he saw the number, he picked up after the first ring.

"Hey, Jen," he said and waited.

Silence on her end. He didn't push her.

"I'm sorry," she said, and it sounded as if she were about to cry.

"Don't be," he said, then set his orange juice down and moved away from the group of people still eating. "Bad night?"

"I keep…seeing it. Over and over."

"I'm so sorry, Jen. What can I do?"

WHAT CAN I DO?

To her, they were four of the most wonderful words in the English language.

"Nothing," she said, leaning back in bed, pulling the covers up to her chin, Shadow burrowing closer. "Maybe I need therapy."

"Maybe," he said. "I've been thinking about some for myself."

"Because of what happened?"

"For a lot of things. But let's get back to you. How can I help?"

"Oh, I don't know. It helps that I can call you and that you aren't mad at me for calling so early."

"Not going to happen." She could hear the affection in his voice, and it warmed her. But she didn't know what to say.

"Actually," Cody said, "your call has helped me make up my mind about something."

"What's that?"

"I was thinking about flying out to L.A. for a few days. I've been putting in long hours since the start of the shoot, so Trevor should let me take a day off. I think there's some stuff he has to shoot that I'm not involved in. I'd like to see you."

"I'd like that, too."

"You got it. Can I call you and let you know as soon as I find out?"

"Yeah." She took a deep breath, then let it out. "I'll keep my cell with me in the kitchen today."

"TREVOR," CODY SAID, WALKING up to his director after he finished the call with Jen.

Trevor looked over at him, a calm and pleased expression on his weathered face. Things were going well, the film would be wrapped within a few weeks. Cody knew that, other than the one day he hadn't reported to work, he'd behaved like a total professional.

"I have a family emergency."

"Your cousin?"

"A woman. The one at the robbery."

"Ah. So she's *become* family."

"She's important to me," Cody said.

"You need some time off."

One of the things Cody liked best about Trevor was the way the man didn't waste time.

"Even just a day off," Cody said.

"I think I could manage two. I can work around you for about forty-eight hours."

"I'd really appreciate it."

"Not a problem. But take care of yourself, Cody. And lay low—they're still playing that damn video."

The *National Star* had been playing the video out in bits and pieces on their nightly news show, building suspense. They still hadn't shown the actual ending but promised it would be spectacular. They'd also been hounding Johnny and his family but so far hadn't been able to locate Jen.

"You can count on it."

SHE'D MADE ALL OF THE chocolate-chip cookie dough and refrigerated it with the intention of baking it early the following morning, so the cookies would be as fresh as possible for Maria's customers, when her cell finally rang.

She picked up, recognizing the Arizona number. "Hey, you," Cody said.

She breathed out a soft sigh of relief.

"Hey."

"Feeling better?"

"Yeah. I've just made three huge bowls of cookie dough and I'm all set for tomorrow."

"Great."

"Do you think I could deliver them to the store?"

She sensed the hesitation in his reply before he said, "Have you been watching television?"

"No."

"They're playing out the video, drawing the whole thing out. I think the ending is going to be shown this Friday. You're still pretty hot on the notoriety scale. I'd lay low."

"Oh."

"Can you bake the cookies and get them to Maria before she leaves? Maybe load her car behind the house?"

"Sure."

"I'd do that. But once I'm out there, I'll teach you some ways to avoid those guys."

She had to laugh at that. "That's one thing I never envisioned myself doing."

"Tell me about it. So, how's your schedule this Monday and Tuesday?"

"Really?" She couldn't keep the delight out of her voice.

"Yeah."

"It's fine." So many thoughts were going through her head, so many emotions at the thought of seeing him again.

"How about we make plans for breakfast on Monday, around eight? I'll come pick you up."

"I'd like that." She also liked the fact that he didn't just assume they were going to sleep together right away. From the sound of his voice, breakfast meant just breakfast.

"Okay. I'm sure we'll talk before then."

She heard some noise off to the side. Voices.

"I've got to go," Cody said.

"Cody? Thanks for this morning."

"I'm here for you, Jen, twenty-four–seven. I want to make sure you know that."

The smile started deep inside her. "I do."

"OH MY *GOD!* CODY ROBERTS, coming *here?*"

Jen looked at her friend with amusement and affection. "Maria, I'm disappointed in you. Here you live in Los Angeles, celebrities come into your coffeehouse all the time, and you're letting a little thing like this throw you."

"*Little thing? Cody Roberts?* Do you *know* what kind of a star he is?" She frowned. "Or was, I guess."

"I just want everything to be normal."

"Should I hide all my DVDs of his movies?" Maria frowned. "I shouldn't ask for an autograph, right? Tacky, huh? Oh my God, *Cody Roberts!*"

"He's just a man, Maria."

"He's just—he's just my favorite action hero of all

time." She hesitated. "Now even more so after he rescued you."

Jen couldn't resist. "What do you know about him, Maria?"

"He's a fantastic actor. I have all his movies on DVD. The one where he really broke through, *The Survivor,* that's in my personal top ten. He always plays these—these *heroes.* The type of guy a woman could look up to—really honorable men, whether they're cowboys or military or soldiers of fortune but always really macho guys. Really straight-up guys but with a sense of humor and a little twinkle in his eye, you know what I mean?"

"Yeah, I think I do. But what do you know about him, the person?"

Maria frowned. "He sort of self-destructed for a while, but word on the street is that he's making this big comeback."

"What happened?"

"He's kind of a private guy, but I did some snooping."

Jen had to smile. Maria lived in Los Angeles, right in the heart of the industry. She knew so many people. If anyone could get to the truth, it was her friend.

"His Dad died. It was a weird accident on the ranch, just a real cruel twist of fate. Cody dropped everything—the film he had in development, *everything*—to get back to his family. Then he came back, but it wasn't pretty."

"What do you mean?"

"He drank a lot, showed up to functions wasted with a—how can I say this delicately?—a certain sort of woman on either arm. I had the feeling he just wanted to numb himself out, he'd been through such an emotionally devastating time. But the press really had it in for him. Called him the bad boy to end all bad boys and said that he had no future in the movies and had wasted his talent. They said he was finished."

"And then?" Jen persisted.

"And then he hit bottom and for a while he just dropped out of sight. Like he'd never existed."

"For how long?"

"Almost two and a half years. An eternity in the business."

"So, you don't know what he did?"

"Nope. I just know that the buzz about his new film is good. And he always seemed like a great guy to me." She took a deep breath. "And now he's coming to *my house!*"

Jen couldn't help laughing. They were sitting at the kitchen table, eating dinner. After finishing up the cookie dough and talking with Cody, she'd walked to the local market and bought enough groceries to make a stew, then spent the afternoon taking a long bath while it cooked slowly in the oven. Shadow had dozed on the bathroom's tiled floor while she'd soaked in the hot, scented water.

"Maria, I want you to do whatever you want to do. Just be natural."

"Is he going to stay here?"

"I don't know."

"You don't know? Oh my *God!*"

"I'm just going to take it easy and see how things go."

"Well, he's obviously interested in you or he wouldn't have set up this date."

"Yeah."

"And he's been phoning you."

She nodded her head.

Maria set down her fork, then pushed her bowl of stew aside and laid her head down on her folded arms, pretending to be overwhelmed. Her voice was muffled as she said, "I have no pride, Jen. Does he have any cute friends?"

Though Jen laughed at her friend's blatant question, she wondered about Cody. Part of her wondered if she knew him at all, if he truly was the man she thought he was.

But another part of her—the stronger part—remembered the man who had taken control of the robbery, who had ensured that she and Johnny had made it out alive. The man who had spent hours with her in a motel room, first making sure she was all right and then making love to her with more passion and intensity than anyone ever had.

Did she know Cody or only a part of him? He was an actor, wasn't he? What if he was only showing her what he wanted her to see?

SHE CALLED LAURA, JOHNNY'S mother, that evening. She'd been thinking about the young cashier and wanted to know how he was doing.

"How nice of you to call and ask after Johnny," she said, and Jen was able to picture Laura all over again, her comforting voice and warm eyes.

"How's he doing?"

Laura hesitated. "He's been having trouble sleeping."

"So have I. I guess it's a common thing after experiencing trauma. Does he dream about it?"

"Yes."

"Please let him know that he can call me at any time if he wants to talk about it." She remembered what Cody had said. "Twenty-four–seven."

"I will. That's so kind of you."

"I mean it."

"I know you do and I thank you for it, Jennifer."

"Is he seeing a therapist?" Jen asked.

"They have their first appointment tomorrow."

"That's great."

"I'm so glad you were able to thank the man who saved your life. The actor?"

"Yes. I did speak to him. I hope it's okay that I gave him your number."

"That was fine. I was so impressed that he cared enough to call and ask about my son."

"That's just the way Cody is."

"You know," Laura said, "Johnny talks about him constantly. I think he wishes he could have been as brave as Mr. Roberts was that day. It's been all over that news show at night, it's almost all they play, and I don't think that helps matters."

Jen thought fast. "You might tell Johnny that we were caught totally off guard, while Cody saw the robber walk inside the store and had time to formulate a quick plan. That's what he told me when I asked him about it."

"That's true. I hadn't thought about it that way.

Jennifer, I think that might help him." She lowered her voice, and Jen assumed someone else was in the house with her. "I haven't been able to watch what's been on TV, but my husband has. He says that Cody almost got himself killed."

Jen's stomach tightened.

"We can never thank him enough. Both my husband and I and our daughter—none of us know how we would've gone on if something had happened to Johnny. It would have destroyed our family."

"I know," Jen whispered.

Laura must have heard something in her voice. "How are you doing, hon?"

"I have my bad moments," Jen admitted. "Mostly just before I go to bed. It hasn't been that long since the robbery, and I have a feeling it's going to take time before I feel totally safe again."

"Of course. I'll let Johnny know he can call you. And I hope he will. I want you to stay in touch with us, all right?"

"I'd like that."

SHE WAS SO NERVOUS THE ENTIRE weekend, she barely slept, thinking about Cody arriving on Monday.

Jennifer kept up a running dialogue in her head as she mixed dough, dropped small mounds on the huge cookie sheets, then slipped them into the commercial oven. She also pulled out the cookbooks she'd brought with her and began to think about other cookies she could incorporate into her business.

"Oatmeal next," she told the four dogs out back, who lazed around on the porch and sometimes came to the back door of the guesthouse and whined their disapproval that she wasn't outside playing with them. "And maybe Snickerdoodles after that."

She tinkered with recipes until they were her own, trying them this way and that. And only when she was satisfied that they were as good as they could get would she write them down in her own personal cookbook.

There was a radio in the commercial kitchen, and she turned it to the classical station. As she baked through the very early mornings, Jen decided that she had one of the best jobs in the world. She could work at her own pace, she was creating something that brought people great pleasure and she could listen to gorgeous music as she did so.

The only thing she couldn't do was let the dogs inside, for obvious reasons.

Maria had gone on and on about how all her customers had raved about the cookies. Jen might have thought her friend was exaggerating, but she'd doubled her order after the first two days, so somebody out there was eating a lot of the cookies she was baking.

The timer beeped, and she turned to take another cookie sheet out of the oven, then glanced up at the clock on the wall.

In a day and a half Cody would be here.

She opened the front door when he knocked and ushered him inside. For a long moment they just looked at each other, then Cody lowered his head and brushed her cheek with a kiss, then pulled her into a hug.

Her arms came up around him and she realized she'd missed touching him. Talking on the phone was one thing, but nothing compared to seeing—and touching—someone.

His scent, the way his clothing smelled so fresh, sent her back to another time, another place, a motel room on the side of the highway in Arizona, where they'd been totally alone.

She was shocked by how powerful the feelings were, how badly she wanted to be alone with him again, to feel those feelings again. But only with Cody.

Jen looked up into his eyes and somehow sensed he was feeling the same thing. Their first time together had been so rushed, so compressed, so intense. How could they start over again from something like that? How could they go out on a normal date, have a normal evening together, with so much sensually intense history between them?

Suddenly she wasn't sure she could find her way in this relationship and she hugged him hard, then stepped away, feeling suddenly shy.

"Maria's in the living room," she said. "I'd like you to meet her."

"Sure," he said. Then he whispered, "But I have to do this first," and kissed her.

When his lips touched hers, it was as if every sensual memory she had of this man rushed back, engulfing her, surrounding her, drowning her. She clung to him, kissed him back, gave him everything she had, trying to tell him without words how much she'd missed him.

And she knew that the chemistry they'd shared in

that motel room hadn't simply been a result of their particular circumstance. It was still there as powerful as ever.

After a time they stepped apart.

She let out her breath, suddenly unsteady, and felt his arm around her, bracing her.

"Maria?" he whispered, and she nodded, then he followed her into the other room.

Maria sat on one of the large couches, trying her best to look composed. And Jen gave her friend credit. Her eyes only widened slightly as she took in Cody.

He greeted her, they shook hands, then he laughed and pulled her into a hug. And Jen realized that he was a man who wasn't afraid to touch people, that his genuine personality was a giving one. She liked him even more.

"I thought you had dogs," Cody was saying as Jen watched him talk with Maria.

"I do. We do. We just have them outside in the backyard because—"

"I'll be hurt if I don't get to meet them," Cody said, a smile in his voice.

"Okay," Maria said and approached the sliding glass door, where Gizmo was barking furiously. Shadow looked nervous, while Kaya and Sheba watched Cody attentively.

All four dogs entered at once, and before a minute had passed, Cody was on the floor with them all, ruffling their fur and not even trying to keep Gizmo out of his lap.

"Which one of these was the vicious killer?" he said, and both Maria and Jen laughed. Sheba was rolled on her back, enjoying a tummy rub, while Kaya had her two front paws over Cody's shoulders from behind as she tried to lick his face. Shadow pressed against Jen's side, but even the Lab puppy made a tentative approach toward their guest.

"I like that the dogs like him," Maria whispered to Jen, and she nodded. Trust their animals to know.

"So," Cody said as he came to his feet, Gizmo in his arms. The little bundle of fur was gazing at him adoringly. "Did you have a place in mind for breakfast? Any special preferences I should know about?"

"I don't know." Jen hesitated. "I guess we should try for someplace pretty private."

Cody turned toward Maria. "What are you up to?"

"Nothing. Monday's my day off."

"We can't leave you here, then," Cody said, and as he turned toward Jen, she saw her friend mouth the words *Oh. My. God!* Jen had to consciously try not to laugh out loud.

"Is that all right with you?" Cody said. "I guess I shouldn't have assumed anything."

"No, it's fine." In a funny kind of way, she would like Maria's company. She knew how she felt about Cody, but she wanted her best friend in the world to have a chance to see what made him so special to her.

She had to know if her impression of him was right and she knew she was too close to him to see straight. Though her heart told her otherwise, her mind insisted on an impartial opinion.

"How are we going to get the two of you out of here—in a trunk?" Maria said. "You weren't followed, were you, Cody?"

He grinned. "No, but unless you want this place to become a madhouse in short order, why don't we take my rental car? Maria, if you go out and get it, Jen and I can get into it in the backyard and lie down until we're well away from your house."

"I love it. My life is a spy novel," Maria said as Cody tossed her the car keys and she went out the door.

"It's the dark green van out front." He turned back toward Jen. "Do you want to take the dogs? I was thinking about this little place on the beach that a friend of mine runs."

"Maria's going to love you forever!" Jen said, then began to assemble all the leashes and collars amid canine pandemonium.

Maria drove the van far back into her driveway so it was hidden in back of her house. Once there, Cody and Jen got in, along with the four dogs.

"Gizmo rides up with me," Maria said, then she shook her head at the sight of them on the floor of the van, the other three dogs sprawled around them.

Cody filled her in on going to his friend's place on the beach. Maria agreed and started up the van.

As they headed out the driveway, Cody was stroking Shadow's head softly, and Jen could tell that her new pet was coming to trust him.

"I'm going to go west on the Santa Monica Freeway. Is that okay?" Maria said.

"Perfect," Cody said. "Then just keep going up Pacific Coast Highway. We'll be stopping a little north of Malibu."

And they were off.

9

IT WAS ONE OF THOSE GLORIOUS Southern California days that made a person remember why they lived in Los Angeles and how wonderful it was to have a beach within driving distance. And Jen thought how different it was from a typical October day in Chicago.

The bright sunlight sparkled on the surface of the Pacific as Maria drove the van north toward Malibu. The beaches weren't as crowded as they were during the summers or weekends, but there were still some people walking along the beach and a few surfers actually braving the waves.

"Whose place is this?" Jen asked, curious about the restaurant.

"Bob's. We met in an acting class. Somewhere along the way he discovered he liked cooking a lot more than acting. So he went to a culinary school and then decided to open a place on the beach." Cody hesitated, glancing at Maria, then back at her. "It's not the fanciest place—"

"That's cool," Maria said from the driver's seat. "Sometimes the places that look like real dumps have the best food."

Cody laughed.

Bob's place was named exactly that. The small restaurant, with a hand-painted sign and a large outdoor patio area, was across the highway from the ocean. As Jen got out of the van in the small parking lot, amid a tangle of leashes and dogs, she admired the way Cody scooped up Gizmo, took Shadow's leash and headed them toward a large table in back, out on the patio.

Maria's shepherds followed at her heels. They were so well trained that they would have done the same off leash, but all of them were aware of Los Angeles's leash laws, so both dogs walked obediently on their leashes.

"Hey, Cody!"

Jen watched as Bob greeted Cody with an affectionate hug. Cody's friend looked like Harry Potter all grown up, with thick dark hair, gentle eyes and black-framed glasses. All that was missing was the scar.

"Bob." Cody turned toward Jen. "I'd like you to meet Jen and Maria. This is Gizmo, this is Shadow and these two are Kaya and Sheba."

"Impressive," Maria whispered at Jen's side, for her ears alone. "He remembered all their names."

"Take that back table," Bob said. "Do all of you like seafood omelets? They're one of the specialties of the house."

"That sounds great," Jen said.

"I'll get menus out to you directly."

THIS AFTERNOON, JEN THOUGHT as she surveyed the empty plates and glasses on the table in front of them, was one of those afternoons that you remembered for the rest of your life. Every element she loved had been present: good food, easy conversation, bright sunlight, lots of laughter. No real hurry to be anywhere or do anything.

The bright October sunshine bathed everyone and everything in its cheerful light. And she was so happy to be with Cody again.

The patio area was charming, filled with colorful flowering plants and a small fountain. The food had been spectacular, the freshest seafood prepared simply and with great care.

She could tell Maria had been very appreciative, seeing the same attention to detail and excellent service that she strove for in her coffeehouse. And it hadn't hurt that Bob and Maria had gotten along like a house on fire, talking and laughing as if they'd known each other all their lives. Something had clicked; if not a romance, then a strong friendship was forming. Trust two foodies to find each other.

And Jen knew that Cody was simply charming Maria. Her friend clearly adored him, laughing at the various stories he'd told them about his current film and asking him endless questions about the actors he'd worked with.

Jen noticed that he went out of his way to show most of his costars in a very favorable light.

"I'm going to take these two for a run along the beach," Maria said, standing up and grasping Kaya's and Sheba's leashes. "Can you watch the Gizmodog for me?"

Gizmo, in Cody's lap, had no intention of leaving. Cody had snuck him some succulent snacks, little tastes of what he was eating, and had made a friend for life.

Shadow was lying at Jen's feet.

"We'll be fine," she said.

As Maria walked away, Kaya and Sheba at her side, Jen thought about how lucky she was to have a friend who was so sensitive to her needs. Even though Cody had invited Maria along, Jen had wanted some time alone with him. Maria had obviously picked up on that.

"She's great," Cody said as they both watched Maria leave.

"I just love her," Jen said. "When I was so confused about what I wanted to do with my life, she didn't even hesitate. She just told me to get my butt out here—but only if I wanted to."

"I'm glad she did."

Cody didn't voice the obvious—that if she hadn't been driving toward Los Angeles on that Arizona highway, they never would have met.

"How are you doing?" Jen said, leaning toward him. "How's the film going?"

"Great. We've hit that place where it just seems to have locked into place, where one day's better than the next."

"How did you get the time off?"

"Trevor told me he could shoot around me for a few days."

"Nice guy," she said.

"The best."

"Do you ever think about it?" she said, knowing he would understand what she was talking about.

"Once in a while." He sighed, then sat back in his chair and tilted his head up toward the sun, closing his eyes. "I think once they stop playing that damn store-surveillance video, it'll be better."

She considered this. "Are you upset with the idea of being called a hero?"

"Aw, it's not that. It's just—anyone would have done what I did."

That surprised her. She reached across the table and touched his hand. Those incredible blue eyes opened and he tilted his head forward and focused that gorgeous gaze on her.

"No, Cody," she said quietly. "Anyone wouldn't have. That's what made what you chose to do so special."

"You think so? I don't know about that."

"Were you scared?"

"Oh, yeah."

"But you did it anyway." She hesitated. "What were you thinking when you came in that door?"

"I wasn't thinking at all, Jen." His hand closed around hers, and she liked the warmth and strength that emanated from him. "That was the strange part. All I could think about was you and that clerk. Johnny. The only thing I knew was that if I didn't do something, one of you might have been hurt. Or worse."

She swallowed against the sudden tightness in her throat. *Or worse.* When she heard Cody's matter-of-fact words, she remembered how she'd felt on that scuffed linoleum floor, staring down the barrel of that shotgun. She remembered the moment when she'd thought her life was over. She laced her fingers through his, almost as if trying to anchor herself.

"I have to apologize to you, Cody."

"For what?" He seemed genuinely amazed.

"For—I thought you were a drunk when you came in that door."

He grinned. "That's called good acting."

She had to laugh. "No, what I mean is, the first thing I thought when you came in that door was that now we have another problem to deal with. I thought of it in reference to me, to the problem I had. I didn't even think that you might have been hurt."

"You're way too hard on yourself. You were racing with adrenaline, just concentrating on survival. Then I come stumbling in the door to make things worse—come on, Jen, I can see how you'd think 'Oh, no, not another complication.'"

"I guess."

"I know so. Don't be so critical toward yourself. It never does any good." He studied her intently, then said, "Whose voice is that? Who was talking to you just now? I can't believe it's you."

She knew what he meant. Where had she learned to be that self-critical?

She laughed self-consciously. "It's my father. He's this very successful businessman and he's totally critical of himself and others."

"That can't be much fun."

"It's not. I guess—I guess it's his voice that I hear in my head a lot."

"Not surprising. Are you an only child?"

"Yeah."

"So you got the brunt of it." Cody considered this, then said, "What did he really think about your coming out here?"

"He's not that happy about it."

"Have you told him that you're on your way to becoming the next Mrs. Fields?"

She laughed again. "I don't think he'd be that impressed."

"What did he think you should do?"

She was touched by the genuine interest in his voice.

"Get married to a suitable man. Help him, support him in his work."

"The corporate wife kind of thing?"

"You got it. Have a few children along the way, and if one of them was a boy and the family business could be turned over to him, so much the better."

Cody considered this.

"But what about your happiness?" he finally said. "Your life? What you need?"

As she looked up at him, their fingers entwined, his gaze locked on hers, Jen thought that she'd never felt closer to a man in her life. He understood. He knew that she'd wanted to find that part of herself that if left undiscovered would have haunted her for the rest of her life.

"I guess...it didn't matter." She thought for a minute, searching for the right words, the honest words, and suddenly felt uncomfortable. Cody didn't rush to fill the silence, and she was thankful. "*I* didn't matter. Cody, I was brought up to see myself in relation to what I could do for others, how I could help them. Be of service. But never to really consider what it was that I was here to do. Does that make sense?"

"Perfect sense." Cody's lips twitched up slightly, and Jen sensed that he was fighting a grin. "Did your Dad have someone suitable all picked out for you?"

"Yes."

"Did you like him?"

"No." She took a deep breath. "I broke off our engagement almost a month before I left. I couldn't pretend anymore that things were fine."

"I can understand that." Cody squeezed her hand. "Has your dad seen the video?"

"Who hasn't?"

He laughed. "Good point. What did he think?"

"He saw it as more evidence that I should get my butt straight home and live the life he wants for me."

Bob came over and unobtrusively filled their coffee cups, then returned to the kitchen.

"I think," Cody said after a long moment, "that he truly thinks that the life he's picked out for you is the best life you could have. I don't think he wants to screw things up for you."

"I don't either," Jen said. "That's what makes it so hard."

"It's tough. And there's no one else to act as a buffer between the two of you?"

"My grandmother did for a while. My mother died when I was young."

"That must have affected your dad."

"He kind of—he went inside himself. It was hard to reach him."

Cody gently pulled her closer, then he kissed the back of her hand and smiled at her. "Give it time. He'll come around."

MARIA CAME BACK ABOUT AN HOUR and a half later, and they decided to have dessert and more coffee.

"Not as good as yours," Maria said decisively as she bit into a chocolate-chip cookie. "Maybe we should talk to Bob about your making some of your cookies for him."

"Great idea," said Cody.

The breakfast crowd had thinned out and the lunch crowd hadn't yet descended, and Bob joined them at their table. And Jen was amazed at how utterly content the man seemed. Bob was one of the lucky ones who had discovered what he had a talent for and was using that talent to its fullest expression.

"Cookies, huh?" he said, studying her, and Jen found that she liked his gentle smile.

"The best!" Maria said. "I took several dozen to my coffeehouse and got absolute raves."

Within five minutes Bob had placed an order, and Jen began to think that she could really make a business out of baking after all.

AFTER THEIR MEAL, CODY DROVE the van farther north, to a secluded beach where the dogs could really run. And they all went down to the water and played in the surf. Shadow really came out of her shell, racing into the surf line to chase the sticks Cody threw into the water for her.

"They're such water dogs, Labradors," Maria said,

watching the yellow Lab swim furiously through the water for the stick.

"She's having a great time," Jen said.

"Aren't we all," Maria said. Then she put her arm around Jen's shoulder and gave her a squeeze. "He's a keeper, Jen. You're one lucky woman."

"I know," she said, watching Cody.

JEN DIDN'T KNOW WHAT WAS going to happen next. She'd been worried thinking about seeing Cody again. Would he rush their relationship? Would he think that just because they'd been totally intimate before, it would be no big deal to be that way again?

She wasn't sure what he wanted. She wasn't even sure what *she* wanted. But all her worry and anxiety seemed to disappear when she saw him again. For some reason, Cody was easy to be with.

He took her hand as they walked along the beach, neither of them saying anything. And once again Maria made herself scarce, going off jogging with her two larger dogs, Gizmo in her arms. Shadow stayed at Jen's heels.

She liked the fact that she and Cody didn't have to talk, that the two of them could be comfortable just walking along the beach and not have to fill the silence with meaningless conversation.

She liked just being with him.

Her heart sped up a fraction as he slipped his arm around her waist.

"Having a good time?" he said.

"Yes." Her arm was around his waist, and she

squeezed him gently. "I'm so glad you could get the time off."

"I had a great incentive," he said, and she laughed.

The beach they were on was practically deserted. They'd walked to the far end of it. They stopped, and Jen looked up at Cody, hoping he would take the moment, make it a little more intimate.

He didn't disappoint her. Lowering his head, he kissed her. And she felt that same peculiar unsteadiness on her feet, so she had to grasp his shoulders to keep from almost spinning away. How one man's kiss could affect her from the top of her head all the way to her toes seemed impossible, but she knew it was real.

Ethan's kisses had been nice but had never moved her like Cody's. And she was suddenly fiercely *glad* that she'd had the courage to move out west and start her life all over again.

He kissed her again, then broke the kiss and steadied her as she laughed, the sound coming out slightly breathy. And looking into those dark blue eyes, she knew that the physical contact had affected him as deeply as it had her.

Shadow, at her side, wagged her tail. It seemed to Jen that her dog had already made up her mind to adore Cody, and the feeling was clearly mutual.

THEY SPENT SEVERAL HOURS ON the beach, walking along the foaming surf, throwing sticks in the shallow ocean for Shadow to chase. Jen was surprised and touched that Cody had stopped by a store long enough to bring some beach towels, a Styrofoam cooler filled with ice and soft drinks and enough sun-screen for all of them.

He'd even brought a box of gourmet peanut-butter dog biscuits for the dogs.

"If you don't want this man," Maria muttered to her while they were drying off their feet and the dogs by the van, "hand him over to me."

Jen only laughed.

SLIGHTLY SUNBURNED AND FEELING relaxed in that way that only a long day at the beach can provide, Cody drove them into Malibu. Maria took all four dogs for a walk in a park, and Shadow was finally confident enough to leave Jen's side for a while.

"It was all that fetch-the-stick earlier," Maria told her. "You both tired her out enough so she's less afraid."

Cody and Jen wandered through a few stores, talking, touching, then stopping for a coffee and split-ting another cookie.

"I'm going to have to try some of yours," Cody said. "After all Maria's told me about them, I'm curious."

"Oh, no! I never sent you that care package! Now there's going to be this huge buildup and you'll prob-ably be disappointed."

"I don't think so. Have you ever considered bak-ing dog biscuits?"

"Gourmet doggie treats? You think there's a mar-ket for them?"

"Oh, yeah. People out here really indulge their dogs. Actually most people do."

"That's a great idea."

"Maria could sell them in her store," Cody said.

"And I have four test subjects." She laughed. "Though I think they'd eat just about anything!"

THEY GOT HOME VERY LATE IN the afternoon, almost early evening. As they approached Maria's house, Jen wasn't sure what it was she wanted. But she knew she didn't want Cody to leave.

"I'm pooped," Maria announced as the van pulled into her driveway and Cody drove it around to the back of the house. "The ocean always does it for me."

"Makes you tired?" Jen said.

"Yep. I'll see you two later."

And with that she got out of the van, whistling for all the dogs. They followed her into the house, a rowdy bunch of paws and tails and sand-covered furry bodies. And Jen knew her friend would clean them all up by herself so she could have more time with Cody.

Jen found herself alone with Cody in the van.

"I don't want you to leave," she said.

"I don't want to."

She yawned.

"You're tired."

She nodded. "All that ocean air."

"Why don't you go take a nap?"

"What will you do?"

"I can crash on the couch, if it's okay with Maria. Or drive home."

This was ridiculous. Cody would understand how she was feeling.

"Were you going to come back tomorrow?"

"You bet."

She took a deep breath. "You could come up to my room."

She saw the definite masculine interest that flared in those blue eyes.

"But could we…just sleep? Would that be okay? I just don't want you to think that I'm playing some sort of game with you—"

He took her hand. "I don't. It's okay, Jen."

SHE LED HIM TO HER BEDROOM, suddenly glad she'd taken the time to make her bed this morning and pick up the clothes that had been draped over various chairs. The queen-size bed looked inviting as Jen drew the drapes to shut out the late afternoon sunlight.

Sitting down on the mattress, she realized she was literally exhausted. She'd been tense about seeing Cody again, worrying if what they'd experienced out in the desert had been some sort of fluke.

And if all the talking they'd done on the phone had been just that—talking. She'd been so scared that when they'd finally be together again things would be—feel—awkward.

She'd been worried about so many things that had come to nothing. Cody was simply Cody. She loved being with him. They seemed to have a connection that went beyond having been in a robbery together and surviving.

"Sand," he said suddenly, taking her out of her thoughts. "I don't want to get sand all over your sheets."

"There's a shower you could use."

"That'd be great."

She showed him which door it was, then lay down on the bed. She thought about joining him, for a moment wanted to, then realized she couldn't expect Cody to not make love to her if they were both wet and naked in a shower stall. That would have been taking things too far, and for whatever reason, she needed more time with him.

He came back into the bedroom within minutes in only his jeans, his hair wet and slicked back off his face, and she remembered another time he'd come out of a shower, in an Arizona motel room.

"I'm going to clean up, too." She kissed him quickly, then said, "You can go ahead and get into bed."

She showered off the sand and sunscreen, rinsing her hair, then toweled off and pulled on clean underwear and an oversized T-shirt she'd brought in with her.

She walked back out into the cool, shadowed bedroom and saw Cody stretched out beneath the flowered comforter and pink sheets. Even among such feminine bed linen, he looked the picture of masculinity.

She slid into bed, still in the T-shirt, and moved closer toward him. And she realized he wasn't asleep, his eyes had just been closed. A large, warm arm came around her, and she felt her body start to relax.

Jen felt safe with Cody next to her, and she laced her fingers through his, resting his hand on the flat of her stomach.

"Just sleep, Jen," he whispered, and the low, masculine sound of his voice seemed to vibrate right through her.

Totally content, she did.

10

JENNIFER WOKE FROM A DEEP, dreamless sleep late that evening. Before she even moved, she heard Cody's voice, so soft in the darkness.

"Jen? You awake?"

"Yeah." She stretched, then turned so she was lying in the bed, facing him. She could barely see his face in the dark, so she turned on the bedside lamp, bathing the room in soft, golden light.

"How're you doing?" he said, and she had to smile. How like Cody to ask—and to really care.

She considered this, then started to laugh.

"I'm starving."

"I was hoping you'd say that. How does dinner sound?"

"Great, but—nothing that will take too much time."

He lay back in bed, considering her request.

"Something fast, something we could get and bring back to the house?" he said. "Or eat there?"

"Perfect."

They left Maria's house under cover of darkness and got into Cody's rental van. Easing out onto Melrose Avenue traffic, a baseball cap pulled down low over his face, Cody headed east until he turned onto La Brea.

"Have you ever been to Pink's?" he said.

"What is it?"

"Best chili dogs in the city."

"Perfect."

The sidewalk stand, with a sit-down area in back, was jam-packed even this late at night, the line at least fifteen people deep. At around eight in the evening, it was dark but not too cold. She and Cody stood in line as she studied the menu.

Every single type of chili dog or loaded hamburger was on the enormous menu, along with several other specialties.

"Clearly you're the expert here, Cody. What do you recommend?"

"I'd start with the classic—a chili dog and a root beer. Then if you're still hungry, I'd go for a side of fries. Then there's always another chili dog if you want to eat a little more."

They'd almost reached the counter, the smells wafting over them mouthwatering. Grilled onions, frying hamburgers, steaming hot dogs and buns and of course the sharp, spicy smell of the chili.

"Cody! How're you doing?" said a stout little Mexican woman, expertly dishing up some chili onto two dogs in one hand.

"Great, Juanita! How's the family?"

Only Cody, thought Jen, *would know each person here as well as their families.*

"Doing okay. Miguel, all he ever talks about is getting into the movies. Do you know of any good acting classes he could attend?"

"I'll give you a terrific coach for him. I'll write

down her number before I leave. Tell her I recommended her, okay?"

"Thanks, Cody! Now, what'll you have? The usual?"

THEY ATE THEIR DINNER AT ONE of the back tables outside, practically in the little parking lot. And it was the best chili she'd had in a long time. It was late enough that, even though the lines were long and the place seemed crowded, they had the back of the patio almost all to themselves.

Jen was beginning to see how carefully Cody had to maneuver in order not to be overwhelmed by the public.

"One false move and we'll end up in the tabloids," he joked. "Though they're much more likely to be outside the clubs by now. I can't see them coming by Pink's except much later for some food."

She liked the fact that he hadn't tried to impress her or rush her into his world. She liked the fact that they were on an ordinary date at a rather extraordinary hot-dog stand in the middle of Hollywood.

And she especially liked that with Cody even a little hot-dog stand felt romantic. He was totally focused on her and what she needed, and that touched her.

She'd finished her chili dog and fries and was halfway done with her root beer when Cody said, "Up for another one?"

"I'm surprised to say that I am."

"We had a late breakfast a long time ago." He stood up. "Anything else?"

"Could we share a piece of that coconut cake?"

"Sure."

As he strode away toward the line in front, she could tell he was happy she was enjoying herself.

She didn't want their evening to end. And when he took her back to Maria's, she was going to ask him to stay.

As Cody ordered the rest of their food, he was happy that Jen was the sort of girl who was comfortable with their going to a neighborhood hot-dog stand.

Of course, eventually he wanted to take her someplace spectacular. But right now speed and good food had been the priorities, and he'd been so grateful she hadn't complained.

She was truly one in a million, and he hoped their evening wouldn't come to an end when he dropped her off.

She asked him to spend the night, then was surprised at how tired she was.

"All that ocean air," he teased, sliding into bed beside her.

"You're not mad that we—"

"Nope." He silenced her with a swift kiss. "Sleep. I'll be here when you wake up, Jen."

She fell asleep with astonishing ease, and Cody knew he would follow her shortly. Jen obviously hadn't been sleeping all that well since the robbery, and if having him in her bed gave her any measure of peace, then he was glad to provide it.

Everything else could wait.

EVEN BEFORE JEN FELT THE warmth of Cody's body beside her in her bed, she realized she'd come awake without flashing back to any memories of the robbery. She felt safe. Secure. All because of the man beside her. And as she came to full wakefulness, she realized what a profound thing he'd done, saving her life. Saving her life and Johnny's with no thought of his own.

She turned over in bed, causing his arm to slide off her, and settled deeper into the bedclothes. She'd glanced at the clock as she'd turned, and it was still quite early in the morning. Baking time.

She had orders to fill.

He was awake, those intense blue eyes taking her in. Jen wondered how long he'd been awake and watching her sleep. She felt disheveled in her T-shirt, her hair all over the place. Pushing it out of her eyes, she whispered, "That's the first good sleep I've had since—since the whole thing."

"Me, too," he said quietly.

"We'll have to sleep together more often," she said, trying for a joking tone.

"Count on it."

His voice sounded rough and gravelly. He was obviously just waking up, as she had. Still, the sound of his voice caused her stomach to do the strangest little flip-flops.

She moved closer to him, slid into his arms and turned her face up to his. "I'd like that."

"The question is," he said and kissed her softly, "what would you like right now?"

"You," she whispered, then felt her body tense

with need as he moved slowly over her, pressing her down into the mattress as he continued to kiss her.

And it was all there again, that strong chemistry. She couldn't claim it was caused by a robbery this time. She couldn't say that they were both so glad to be alive that every sense each of them had was heightened.

They were together again in the most intimate way possible, and it was just the two of them alone in the world, alone in this bedroom, this bed, at this time, together.

She'd always needed a lot of time when it came to sexual matters, so Jen was astounded at how swiftly she was ready, how quickly she wanted him, how eager she was.

"Now," she whispered, yearning to have him even closer, so beautiful, so powerfully male, so sexual.

"Sure?" he whispered.

"Yeah," she said, threading her fingers through his hair and pulling his mouth down to hers. She, who had never been that aggressive in her sexual life, felt safe enough with this man to demand, to insist, to persuade and even take the lead.

Then he was part of her, deep inside her, and the moan of sheer, unadulterated pleasure that escaped her surprised her so much, she started to laugh.

"I hope that means you like this," he whispered in her ear, then kissed her temple.

"Mmm," she sighed and gave herself up to pure pleasure.

"ARE YOU HUNGRY?" SHE SAID.

"I could eat," he said. "And I'm beginning to see a theme to this relationship. You?"

She nodded. "Am I that big a pig?"

"Never. We just burned up a lot of energy. Want to try going out again?"

He was going to leave it up to her.

"What do you think?" she said.

Cody stretched, and she watched the way his muscles moved beneath his skin. He was simply a beautiful man, larger than life. He had whatever requisites a movie star required, one of the main ones being that you simply couldn't take your eyes off him.

"I think we could chance it, especially if we go to a place that's a little out of the way."

She started to slide out of bed. "You're on."

THEY WENT TO A SMALL LOCAL coffee shop for breakfast, and the waitress was so tired, she didn't care who Cody was. Jen found herself amazingly hungry and ordered one of the specials—bacon and eggs and pancakes and hash browns. Cody did the same.

The day was an absolutely ordinary one for her, yet because Cody was there, it was extraordinary. He came back to Maria's with her, and as she'd mixed up extra bowls of cookie dough in anticipation of his visit, all she had to do was take the small scoop and line up the balls of dough on the various cookie sheets, then bake them.

He kept her company the entire time.

They never seemed to run out of things to talk about. Once Maria had come into the commercial kitchen and picked up her boxed order, Jen washed her hands, cleaned up the kitchen and told Cody they had the rest of the day to themselves.

"What would you like to do?" he said.

"Anything?" she replied, deciding to tease him a little.

"Anything," he said.

"Well, let's go upstairs while I change clothes and get cleaned up, then we can decide."

She took his hand and led him out of the commercial kitchen, into Maria's house, where all the dogs were snoozing on the living room floor, then upstairs to her room.

"What would you like to do?" she called from the bathroom.

The slight pause told her everything she wanted to know, but he said, "Whatever you want, Jen. The day's yours."

She loved him for that.

Deciding to surprise him, she stripped down to her underwear and came out of the bathroom. He was sitting on her bed and she had just a moment to register the surprise on his face before she sat in his lap.

"I thought," she whispered, "that we both might come up with a few ways of entertaining ourselves."

"Hmm," he said, and she loved the feel of his hands as they came around her waist, steadying her.

"What do you think?" she said, then traced the outline of his lips so softly with one of her fingers.

"I don't know," Cody replied. "I hear there are a few good movies out."

She almost laughed out loud. The reaction his body was giving her was at complete odds with the idea of going out to see a movie.

"How about—" she said as she got up, then straddled his jean-clad legs "—if we talk a little more about what we might do." She couldn't believe she felt safe being so bold with him.

Rising up so he had a clear view of her lingerie-clad body, she leaned against him and kissed the side of his face, then took his earlobe between her teeth and gently bit down—

And was flat on her back in the midst of the rumpled bedclothes before she'd had time to blink.

"Wow. That was fast." She laughed as he stood up and began to shed his clothing.

"As the saying goes," Cody said, lowering himself onto the bed, "you ain't seen nothing yet."

IT WAS THE SAME AS IT ALWAYS was with them, that profoundly powerful sexual pull. That same frantic quality to their lovemaking that was partially satiated when they were finally coupled, and then rose and fell in intensity. She surrendered to it, knowing that she would let him do whatever he wanted, that he would never hurt her, that he would only bring her great pleasure, then peace.

"Anything else planned for the day?" Cody said.

"Nope."

"The dogs are okay?"

"They stay in the living room, lying in the sun. And they have a dog door to the backyard."

"This gets better and better," he said, kissing her neck. "What time does Maria get home?"

"She's working a double shift today. She won't be home until around nine."

He slid his hand slowly up and down her bare back, and the strong motion comforted her, relaxed her, then aroused her. She didn't stop him as he slid between her legs and entered her, starting up that irresistibly sexual rhythm all over again.

THEY MADE SANDWICHES IN THE kitchen for lunch and carried them up to her bedroom, but around five in the afternoon Cody decided that they had to do something for dinner.

"Like, get out of bed, I mean," he said, teasing her.

She lay back in her bed, totally satiated. No one had ever made love to her the way Cody had, and she was still feeling the wonderful, voluptuous little aftershocks.

"Shower?" he said.

"Together?"

"The only way."

She frowned playfully. "You know we won't get much showering done."

"I just have this thing about seeing you covered in bubbles. Can you humor a poor boy?"

She laughed and took his hand as he headed toward the shower.

ALMOST AN HOUR AND A HALF later they went out for dinner.

The place Cody picked was a little Italian restaurant on Third Street, and the elderly couple who owned it welcomed him like a long-lost son. They showed them to a table far in the back, with promises that if things became too public, they would let them eat in the kitchen, at their table.

"It must be strange," Jen said after their salads were served.

"The fame thing? You get used to it. I don't really feel like I can complain because it comes with the territory."

"Anything you can't stand?"

"I'll always sign autographs, but after a meal. For a while it got to the point where I couldn't finish eating anything, I was so busy signing."

"Hmm." She considered this, wondering what it would be like to live your life out in a glorified fishbowl for everyone to see.

"It's okay. The people here are great."

Their pasta dishes arrived, and Jen could have sworn they'd been transported to Italy. She'd spent several summers in Europe with her father, and the dishes that had been prepared for them tonight rivaled anything she'd tasted there.

"This is really excellent."

"Victor and his wife know how to cook," he said. "And you've got to try some of my pasta." It struck Jen that he was enjoying watching her take pleasure from their dinner, he liked seeing her enjoy her food. Again she was struck by the fact that he was such a generous man.

"How did you meet them?" she said as he spooned a generous taste of his pasta dish onto her bread plate.

"They used to run a pizza stand, selling whole pies and by the slice. It was great food, and there were a few times when a slice of that pizza was all I could afford for dinner."

"I'll bet you were glad when that changed."

Cody grinned. "They say the days you're struggling are the most fun, and in some ways they are. You're more innocent, you don't know as much about the business end, the reality of it. But I always try to make the present moment the most fun."

"You're a lot of fun," she said and couldn't keep the smile from her face, especially when she remembered their shower together.

"Good," he said and poured her another glass of wine.

They lingered over their dinner, enjoying each other, the ambiance of the restaurant, the wine and then they shared dessert, a sinfully rich tiramisu.

Afterward they went back into the kitchen, and Cody surprised her again by talking with the couple in Italian. She knew enough of the language that she could follow the gist of the conversation.

"I'm impressed," she said as they walked to the car. The Los Angeles night was cool, with a slight breeze. Perfect weather. People were out walking, but no one bothered them.

"Don't be. I pick up languages so easily, it's ridiculous. I once worked on a movie in Prague and I was speaking Czech before I knew what was happening."

Jen remained quiet as he opened the passenger-side door of the rental van and helped her inside, then watched as he walked around to the driver's side. While he'd been talking with the older Italian man, she'd made conversation with his wife. The woman had revealed the fact that when Cody had made it big, he'd been the main silent backer in their expansion from a pizza stand to a full-scale Italian restaurant.

The more she discovered about Cody, the more she liked him.

He drove up the driveway and around to the back of the house, parked the van, then came around to her side of the car and opened her door.

"So," he said as he shut the passenger side door. "I should be heading back to the airport."

"How soon do you leave?"

"My flight's around two in the morning—it's always less crowded that way, less of a hassle."

She couldn't let him go just yet.

"Come upstairs with me," she whispered. "We still have a little time."

"Jen, you don't have to—"

"I know I don't. I want to."

Taking his hand, she started toward the house.

IN HER BEDROOM THEY REMOVED each other's clothing at lightning speed, quietly now, conscious of the fact that Maria was probably home and already asleep.

But before they hit the bed, Cody took both her hands in his, stilling her.

"I wasn't thinking very straight that day out at the motel, Jen, or earlier today," he whispered. "I know it's ridiculously late to bring this up, just insane. But I need to ask you—what about birth control?"

"It's okay. We're safe."

"You're using something?"

"Yes." She took a deep breath, let it out. "I should ask you about…if there's anything I need to know—Oh, I hate this. I mean, disease—"

"Just had a physical for the film. I'm fine."

"Me, too."

"Now that that's out of the way," he said, swinging her up into his arms, "let's get down to the good stuff."

THE GOOD STUFF WAS GREAT.

It felt to Jen as if they'd been making love for years instead of this being so early in their relationship. There was none of the awkwardness, none of the hesitation or tension that had always been a part of other encounters.

He made her feel so safe. So wanted. So cherished.

There was that same urgency this time, a level of arousal in both of them that precluded a lot of foreplay. She was almost embarrassed at how quickly they just got down to it again and then she forgot her embarrassment as she could only feel and surrender to waves of sensation. She felt as if that first time with Cody she'd been so open, so emotional and raw that she hadn't held back. She'd given him everything, and nothing was different this time or the last.

He pulled her to his side, kissed her forehead, then her mouth, then held her tightly against him.

"I wasn't coming out here looking for this," he whispered into the darkness once he'd gotten his breath back.

"Yeah, yeah," she whispered back, then laughed as his fingers gently dug into her side.

"Uh, maybe a little. When it's this good, it's irresistible."

Her hand rested on his flat stomach and she smoothed her fingers over the strong muscles. "You won't get any argument from me."

"Can I see you when I come back?"

Happiness seemed to sing in her bloodstream and she felt as if she were light and free, her entire body relaxed.

"Yes. I'd like that a lot."

He stroked her hair as he talked, his voice low.

"I should be done with filming right before Halloween. We should be able to think up something fun to do that weekend."

"And how nice for you," she said, a hint of laughter in her voice, "that you'll be disguised in a costume."

"I was thinking the same thing."

He was stroking her stomach, just gently touching her, and she already felt the stirrings of arousal, sharp and insistent, her muscles jumping slightly beneath his hand.

He seemed to catch that arousal, drawing her up on top of him so she straddled him.

"I have the best view in town," he whispered before he kissed her.

"You think so?" She found that she loved to tease him.

"I know so." He glanced at the bedside clock. "This one will have to be quick."

"Whatever you want," she whispered as she leaned down to kiss him.

SHE WOKE UP THE NEXT MORNING very early when her alarm went off and felt fantastic.

Cody had left late the night before, just in time to get to the Burbank airport and catch his plane. She'd hated seeing him go, but he'd kissed her warmly, promised to call, then had left.

Jen found that she'd had to make a very conscious effort to fall back asleep after he'd left. Their two days together had played through her mind until she'd made an effort to slow her breathing, stop thinking and finally sleep.

She felt a distinct weight at her feet and knew it was Shadow. Maria had probably let her out of her room when she'd heard Cody's car leave.

"Hey, sweetie," she said, ruffling the Lab's head. "You loved playing in the ocean, didn't you?"

The puppy wagged her tail, and Jen kept petting her, scratching her behind her velvety ears.

"We're going to have to make that a weekly event, you and the Pacific. Okay?"

Shadow wiggled closer.

"I've got to take a shower and get downstairs to that cookie dough. So you be a good girl, and I'll play with you later."

SHE BAKED UP THE COOKIES AT record speed, loving the ease and convenience the commercial ovens gave her. Maria walked in when the first few batches were done, a smile on her face.

"I'm going to be very good and not ask for any of the details. But I don't even have to ask, 'cause I can see the smile on your face, you lucky girl!"

Jen started to laugh as she boxed up the cookies. "No details, just that I'm very happy."

"When's he due back?"

"The film wraps just before Halloween. He said we'd have to think of something fun to do for that weekend."

"I have just the thing," Maria said as she reached for the first large box of cookies. "I'm going to get a great band in to play Halloween night, and everyone who comes to see them has to wear a costume. Would you and Cody be up for it?"

"Oh, try and keep us away!"

CODY LOVED THE IDEA.

"Okay, so we have to start working on our costumes."

Jen laughed. "This has to be the actor in you!"

"No, this is the director in me. I have some great connections for costumes, so if we know what we're going as early enough, I can get us some great stuff."

"Masks would be good," she said.

"I'd agree."

The video of the robbery on the tabloid TV show had finally played out to its end, but even by the end of the month, things probably wouldn't have died down. The various tabloids were still milking this incident for all it was worth.

"How about Zorro?" she said. "Now there's a mask!"

"Nah. No one does it better than Antonio Banderas."

"Have you ever met him?" She had to ask.

"Yeah. Once. At Cannes. He's a really nice guy."

"Okay. No Zorro."

"Why don't you tell me what you'd like me to be?" Cody said, and her heart sped up at the thought of seeing him as any character she wanted him to be.

"Hmm. This could be interesting."

"Your wish is my command, Jen."

"Well, I've always kind of had a thing for—no, you'll think it's silly."

"No, I won't. Trust me."

She hesitated, then said, "A pirate."

"Yo ho, yo ho, a pirate's life for me!"

She laughed again as he sang the familiar refrain from Disney's *Pirates of the Caribbean.*

"Now, what will you go as?" Cody said. "Something to complement my pirate's outfit. Perhaps a pirate's wench?"

"There were female pirates," she said.

"We could go as a pair of pirates."

She thought about it for a split second, then realized she didn't want to wear pants but something softer, more feminine. A skirt of some sort, with lots of tiers—

"A Gypsy. I'm going as a Gypsy. But I'm not going to rent a costume. I'm going to make one and surprise you."

"I'm impressed. You sew?"

"Of course."

"A Gypsy." He was silent for a while, and Jen could tell he was thinking about this. "Okay. But with one condition."

"What?"

"You have to read my palm and tell me my fortune—damn it, I've got to go, they're calling for me."

"'Bye," she said, then as soon as she hung up, she began to think about her costume.

She wanted to knock his socks off.

"A PIRATE, HUH?" MARIA SAID the following evening as they had dinner together. "He should look just great—and he could wear a mask and not be seen."

"My thoughts exactly."

Maria was full of ideas about the big Halloween party at her coffeehouse. She wanted to pull out all the stops to thank her customers for their loyalty during her first year of business.

Jen never tired of hearing Maria discuss everything from the placement of the band to the food she was going to order in to the dozens of cookies she wanted to have and the plants she was going to use to transform the decor.

And her costume. "I'm going as that girl Nicole Kidman played in *Moulin Rouge*—one of those dancers."

Maria had just the figure to pull it off, along with the attitude.

"Pumpkin cookies," Jen said suddenly. "I could make pumpkin chocolate-chip cookies."

"Perfect! Now if you can just help me select which plants will survive where, I'll be ready for the weekend. Well, as ready as I'll ever be!"

JEN KNEW HOW TO SEW, AND MARIA had a great machine, so she decided to go all out. After asking Maria where the nearest fabric store was, she headed out with just the idea in her mind.

Once there, she looked through the pattern books endlessly until she found the dress she wanted. Then it was on to material—she'd decided to make the low-cut top a different color than the skirt and took her time choosing just the right material. Then thread, buttons, hem tape...

The woman at the checkout counter recognized her.

"You're the girl from the robbery!" she said loudly enough so that other customers turned and stared.

Jen had thought about what she would do if anyone recognized her. She had her answer all locked and loaded.

"No, but I look just like her, everyone keeps telling me that."

"Oh my God, wasn't that something, the way that Cody Roberts went right in there and saved those two? Talk about a real hero!"

"He was amazing," Jen said quietly. She paid for her purchases as quickly as she could, with cash, and left.

THE FROTHY TIERED SKIRT WAS to be black with red trim, the peasant-style blouse a deep red. Jen found sewing a pleasant way to pass the afternoons, especially as she thought about Cody and his reaction to her costume.

She had some gold hoop earrings she could wear and she was making a scarf out of a small piece of the black material that she could tie around her head. Maria had even offered to lend her a deck of tarot cards so she could truly tell Cody his fortune.

"He wants me to read his palm," Jen said one night at dinner.

"I've got some great books on palmistry. That stuff works. You could read up on it and really scare him."

They both laughed at the thought of that, but when Jen came back in from baking the following morning, she found several books from Maria's extensive library on her nightstand by the bed.

Intrigued, she opened one.

"Almost done," Cody said early one evening. Jen was touched that he'd called early because of the fact that she was up before sunrise most mornings to get her baking done. Even earlier than his day began.

"Do you like the way it's coming out?"

"Actually I do. I'm not one of those actors who can't stand to see dailies—and what I've been seeing from everyone is pretty damn good."

"Great."

"We're not talking Oscar material here, but it's a solid film, just sheer entertainment."

"I can't wait to see it."

"You'll have to come to the premiere with me," he said.

She didn't answer as she thought of what that would mean. Truly entering Cody's world. Photographers, directors, other actors. The public eye.

"Would you want to go?" he said, and she could hear the note of caution in his voice.

Honesty. Always with Cody nothing but honesty.

"I'd be a little scared. It's kind of out of my comfort zone. But if you told me what to expect so I didn't embarrass you—"

"Never. Don't even go there. Jen, we could go and just have a great time. But don't feel that you have to if you don't want to."

She snuggled back against her pillows. "I'd be okay if I was with you."

"I wouldn't let anything happen to you."

"I know that." She closed her eyes. "I miss you, Cody."

She heard his sigh. "Me, too. I miss being with you."

"Do you ever wonder about the way we were kind of thrown together?" she said.

"No."

"You don't? Not at all?"

"I just try to take life as it comes. I used to question everything, and it made me crazy."

"Hmm. I guess I'm still in the questioning stage."

"We would've gotten together, robbery or no robbery."

"You think so?"

"I *know* so."

She considered this, liking the determination she heard in his voice. "What do you know that I don't?"

"I know that I saw you entering that convenience store and I thought you were really cute, but I didn't think that you'd talk to a guy like me."

"What are you talking about, a guy like you? What does that mean?"

"I wasn't at my best."

"In what way?"

"I'd been having a kind of wild weekend."

"Ah. But you wanted to talk to me?"

"You don't want to know what I thought."

"Oh, yeah, the male mind."

Cody just laughed.

"So you saw me go into the store?"

"Yep. Saw you start toward the coffee. I was going to go on in and try to talk with you, when I saw…that guy."

Jen was silent, remembering. Then, deciding she didn't want to remember certain things, she deliberately changed the subject.

"What would you have done if there hadn't been a robbery?"

"I would've gotten my sorry ass in there and tried to convince you that there was a genuinely good man underneath all that scruffiness, nothing a good shower wouldn't have cured."

She laughed.

"You probably would've kicked me to the curb," he said.

"Now you sound like Dr. Phil. He's from Texas, too, isn't he?"

"Yep. Texas born and bred."

"Do you ever wonder why it happened the way it happened?" she said, her voice very soft.

"Yeah. Sometimes." He hesitated. "Why? Do you think things are going too fast?"

"Sometimes I do and then other times I don't. Usually I think that things are happening between us just the way they're supposed to."

"I know what you mean."

"I feel so close to you, Cody, and then sometimes I think it's just a reaction to everything that's happened."

"Yeah. I know."

"Like the Stockholm syndrome or something."

"Now hang on a minute—that's when you're kidnapped."

"But the stress thing, the unusual incidents. You know what I mean."

"Yeah, I do." He hesitated, then said, "Jen, the only thing I know is that as soon as this film is finished and I can come home to you, I'd like to spend enough time with you to know what's really going on between us. Is that okay with you?"

"I'd like that," she whispered, her throat suddenly unbearably tight.

"Don't get scared. Don't get all worried. I've always gone with my gut, and my gut tells me that we would've gotten together, robbery or not. Some things are just meant to be."

"I know," she said. For one long, silent moment, she had an overwhelming urge to tell him that she loved him. But it couldn't possibly happen this fast, could it?

"Jen," he said, and the way he said her name made her melt.

"Yeah?"

"I'm not going to say the words right now because I have the feeling they might scare you off. But I have strong feelings for you, and they have nothing to do with the way we got together so fast. Do you know what I mean?"

"Yeah," she said, her eyes filling as she struggled to keep her voice steady.

"So," Cody said, and she could almost feel the apprehension in his voice. "I may be this big actor in the tabloids, but here in real life, with you, I'm just a guy. So can you find it in your heart to put this guy out of his long-distance misery and let him know if he's got a chance?"

"Much more than a chance," Jen said, reaching for a tissue, wiping her eyes. "But you know that."

"Not just that Stockholm syndrome?" he said.

"No. But how can it be this right this fast?"

"I don't know. Sometimes it just is."

She thought back to that morning on the floor of the convenience store and of all the things she'd believed were over for her. And of how terrified she'd been. But even more than losing her life, she'd been so afraid that she'd never really live it.

How could she still be afraid? Didn't that mean that she was still refusing to really live?

"Cody," she whispered.

"Yeah?"

"I think I'm falling in love with you."

"Ah, Jenny," he said softly. "You took the words right out of my mouth."

11

TIME SEEMED TO RACE BEFORE the Halloween party at Maria's coffeehouse, and there never seemed to be enough of it to get everything done. Before Jen knew it, she was driving toward the Burbank airport very early on the morning of Halloween to pick up Cody. Filming had gone a little later than he'd expected, but now he was finished with the movie and more than ready to come home.

At one in the morning there wasn't too much traffic on the freeway, but Los Angeles could truly be called one of the cities that never slept. Jen had insisted on picking Cody up, and as she drove she realized she finally felt comfortable driving in the city. She'd reached one of those moments after a move when she didn't have to consciously think about where she was going. She just drove.

She was a worrier by nature, and part of what had been unnerving her was the fact that she and Cody had been getting along so well. But she knew that what they had so far was more of a private relationship, conducted by phone and inside Maria's home. They hadn't yet gone public, and she knew that this would throw a considerable challenge her way.

Though she wasn't looking for trouble, she had her doubts. She wondered if she was strong enough to enter that part of Cody's life. And she wondered how the two of them would fare once their relationship went public. He was one of the most recognized faces on the planet, and she had always been a private person.

Though Cody had always been confident they would have met no matter what, sometimes Jen wondered.

And she wondered if she truly knew what she was getting into. When she was with Cody or talking with him on the phone, she had no worries. It was only late at night, alone, or at odd moments during the day that she worried or had any doubts at all.

She entered the airport, headed toward parking, stopped and had her trunk searched, then parked the car and went inside the main area of the small airport.

She couldn't wait to see Cody. They'd talked a lot on the phone since the one call when she'd told him she'd loved him and he'd answered in kind, but this was the first time she would be seeing him since that confession.

It had happened so *quickly* between them. On top of that fact, this relationship was something she hadn't counted on. She'd come out west to find herself, not necessarily a relationship. But it had certainly found her.

In her mind, in the plans she'd made when she'd thought about reinventing her entire life, the relationship would've come *after* she'd been more established in her life out here. She'd thought it might happen a year after her arrival, when things in her life were more firmly in place.

But Jen had come to realize that life didn't always work out that way. It was like that John Lennon quote: "Life is what happens when you're busy making other plans." That was certainly what had happened to her and to Cody.

She saw him coming toward her from the restricted area and she waved, suddenly feeling ridiculously happy. He caught sight of her, smiled, and the emotional force of that smile seemed to almost knock her off her feet.

When she was with him, she had no doubts.

He reached her, swept her up into a hug, then a kiss. Any doubts she might have had about where they were both going with the relationship evaporated in that moment. As she kissed him, as she caught that scent that was his alone, he filled her world for that moment, and she let him, gloriously happy.

HE HAD TWO BAGS THAT HE'D checked, and once he'd slung them off the luggage carousel and they made their way to the parking lot, Jen began to relax.

A few people had recognized him, but either Burbank was too laid-back an industry town or it was just too early in the morning for anyone to work up much enthusiasm for spotting another movie star. Once on their way out of the parking lot and to the main street, Jen felt completely relaxed.

She'd eventually have to come to terms with Cody's fame and what that brought to her life.

Her father was well known in his business world,

but it wasn't the sort of fame that Cody had. She'd watched as people stared at Cody from afar, then tried to work up the nerve to approach him, touch him, ask for an autograph or tell him how much one of his movies had meant to them.

But once they talked to him, he quickly reassured them that he was just a man, just a person, just as they were. And Jen watched another curious phenomenon—some people accepted this and some just couldn't. Some wanted Cody to stay firmly in the role of larger-than-life and couldn't seem to accept that he was just a man who had an extraordinary job.

There were times, she thought as they drove along on the freeway, when she was glad she hadn't recognized him when they'd met. She glanced at him in the passenger seat, the seat angled back, his head tilted back on the headrest, eyes closed.

"Tired?" she said.

"A little. There were a lot of loose ends to tie up today."

Making movies looked glamorous from the outside, but if you had even the slightest look into what really went on, you learned it was a job like any other. A creative job, and one that Cody obviously loved, but a lot of work.

"I think people only see the ninety minutes to two hours of story on the screen," he'd once said to her. "They think that's all there is—that and the premieres. They don't see all the work it takes to get there, all the people and all the work it continues to take."

She didn't say anything more to Cody, just let him rest as she drove, until they reached Maria's house.

She pulled into the driveway and all the way around in back, expecting the house to be still and silent at this time of night.

The huge Halloween party would take place this same day, in the evening. Maria was in the last-minute stages of planning the entire thing, making sure all was perfect at A Bit of a Buzz. Jen had been sure her friend would want to get a good night's sleep, so she was a little surprised to see the lights still on inside.

She grabbed Cody's duffel bag out of her trunk, he shouldered the rest and they headed inside to hear Maria in the large kitchen, talking on the phone, clearly upset.

Jen glanced at Cody, sure he was exhausted from his long day, but his attention was already on her friend.

"What's going on?" he said.

"I don't know."

"I'm going to take these upstairs. I'll be right back down." And with that he went up the stairs. None of the dogs barked or caused a ruckus. It said a lot about Cody that the animals didn't feel he was a stranger or was intruding into their household. He was simply one of Maria's huge extended family of friends, and they accepted him as such.

Once Cody came back downstairs, they both went into the kitchen in time to see Maria set the receiver down, then put her head into her hands.

"What happened?" Jen said.

"What's *not* happening." Maria took a deep breath. "Problems with the caterer. I wish I'd never hired these people!" She glanced up and saw Cody. "Hey, Cody, good to see you."

"What can we do?" Cody said, and Jen loved the way he embraced other people and their problems. He was a man who wasn't afraid to get his hands dirty, to get involved. That generous spirit she so admired was in action again. Cody was her hero in so many countless little ways.

"What can you do?" Maria laughed. "Find me more food."

"You're kidding, right?" Jen said.

"Nope. I'm just afraid these people aren't going to come through. I can't understand why they were so highly recommended."

"Do you need something fancy?" Cody said.

"What do you have in mind?"

"Pizza," Cody replied, and Jen flashed back to their dinner out, the elderly Italian couple they'd talked with and the wonderful food they'd shared.

"Pizza," Maria said, "would be fine."

CODY WAS AS GOOD AS HIS WORD. Later that same morning, as soon as he knew the restaurant was open, he made a phone call, then told Maria she could have as many of the savory pies as she wanted. He'd even go pick them up.

"Does this guy have a brother?" Maria wanted to know. Jen had to laugh. She was doing some of the final decorating in the coffeehouse, adding those last few touches and doing her best to calm her friend down. Maria was having last-minute jitters at the thought of throwing a huge blast.

"No. But I think he has a cousin—back in Texas. He raises horses."

"You're one lucky woman," Maria said again, then went back to waiting on a customer. One of the reasons A Bit of a Buzz had been such a success so far was her attention to every single detail.

There wasn't a customer who came in who didn't feel that Maria gave him or her exquisite attention. In this day and age of sloppy, uncaring service, it made a huge difference.

Jen smiled as she continued to string more lights. At the last minute, Maria had brought in more small pumpkin lights, and she was placing them strategically around the shop.

"With my luck, the band will cancel," her friend said.

"Stop with the disaster mentality. I think you've had all the last-minute surprises you're going to have with the caterer, and Cody solved that problem."

Cody had dropped into her bed last night after talking with Maria, and Jen had watched him sleep. Clearly exhausted, he'd needed the few hours rest, and she'd been glad he felt comfortable enough with her to not feel he had to offer up some kind of explanation as to why they weren't getting intimate right away.

She hadn't worried at all. In her experience, the feeling between two people was either there or it wasn't, and no amount of lovemaking could force a feeling into existence when it wasn't naturally there.

With Cody, from the moment she'd seen him at the airport, all those feelings had been there.

She hadn't woken up at the same time with him this morning. She'd slipped out of bed early, while he'd still slept, and started baking more cookies for tonight's party. She'd left him a note and let him sleep in, which he had, but the moment his feet had hit the floor, he'd become a troubleshooter for Maria, helping her with various problems.

She'd wanted more plants moved to the coffeehouse, and he'd complied. Some of the larger ones that had been out back had been moved in late this morning, as Cody had called his friend Bob, who had taken time away from his restaurant to help.

Bob had brought down his pickup truck and both men had moved more plants in, then rearranged the ones that were already there to Maria's frenzied and exact expectations. Cody had even hammered in a few nails so Maria could hang a few more pictures on the walls.

Jen had been so impressed that there had been no complaining on Cody's part. Most men might have made a few sarcastic remarks or even refused to help at all. Cody seemed to emotionally understand that Maria was under a lot of pressure and one of the ways she blew off steam was to second-guess herself a lot.

Jen also noticed a little bit of chemistry between Bob and Maria—the two foodies—though her friend was doing her best to hide it. Maria had major trust issues to surmount because of her last boyfriend, but Jen had a feeling that Bob liked her and was intrigued with her enough that he would have the necessary desire to break down some of those barriers. Time would tell.

"I can help with that," a familiar voice behind her said.

She glanced in back of her to see Cody, sweaty and

dirt stained, in worn jeans and a T-shirt. He smiled down at her, and everything inside her sped up, that little tingle of excitement shot through her and made her body feel so alive.

"I could use your height," she admitted.

"You got it."

They worked in a companionable silence for a while, hanging the rest of the pumpkin lights and then checking with Maria to see that they had arranged them just so.

"Then you'll be picking up the pizzas at around six?" Maria said to Cody.

Jen had to hide her smile. In the beginning Maria had been so intimidated about meeting Cody, about his coming to her house and entering her life. Now she treated him like a member of the family. It amused Jen, but she knew she couldn't let Maria know how she felt. At least not now, hours before her big night.

"You got it. Bob and I will take care of it. Anything else you need done around here?"

"Nope," Maria said. "We're just about ready—"

"Cody Roberts, I have a bone to pick with you!" A heavyset blond woman stuffed into a navy jacket and skirt and tottering in very high heels barreled past Jen, almost knocking her over in her haste to get to Cody. He reached out, and Jen felt his hand on her arm, steadying her.

"And who said I might be that man?" Cody replied in an absolutely flawless Irish accent. Jen watched, amazed, biting her tongue against the laughter that threatened to bubble up out of her.

"You're not?" This stopped the woman in her tracks.

"No. Colin's the name. But you know, now that you mention it, my mum used to tell me how much I looked like the lad. I saw a few of his movies, and, being a wise boy, I took it as a compliment." He smiled down at her, and the woman gazed up at him, puzzled.

"But you look *just* like him," she said, clearly not able to put all this together.

"That I do, and I thank you for the compliment. Now, is there anything we can be doing for you—a nice cup of coffee or something like that? I hear the raspberry scones are quite good this morning. How about one on the house?"

"I, well, Colin… I suppose—"

Cody was already in action, striding over to where Maria was behind the counter watching him with amusement in her eyes. Without a word she handed him a scone on a plate, along with a fork and a napkin.

"Here you go, ma'am," Cody said, steering the large woman toward a table in the sunlight, right by a window. "And you're sure you'll not be wanting a cup of coffee? The best in the city, if I do say so myself."

"A latte?" she said weakly, and to Jen it seemed as if the woman still didn't know what had hit her.

"I'll bring it right over," he said, winking at Maria, who busied herself making the brew. "Now, what is it that you wanted to tell this rascal, Mr. Cody Roberts, the movie star?"

Jen couldn't take her eyes off him. He'd never looked more attractive to her, in his work clothes, all sweaty and covered with dust. It was that devilish twinkle in his eyes, the way he was enjoying this prank.

"Just that, well, I thought you were him and I wanted to yell at you and ask you why you hadn't had a movie out in such a long time. I mean, I'll go and see anything that guy is in!"

"Sure, and I know what you mean. My sisters have the same reaction to the man. It's madness. They practically have to go to confession directly after the matinee. But I heard—well, don't you go repeating this, but I think this little bit of news will please you."

"Not a word," the woman said, then took a bite of her scone, dusting the crumbs off the front of her suit jacket.

"You know how this is an industry town and everyone's always talking. The rumors and such."

The blond woman nodded her head, and Jen had to look away from this particular scene to keep from laughing.

"I hear he's just finished another movie, and the inside word on it is that it's *very* good. That Trevor— that British director—he's a bloody genius, don't you think? It should put Cody right back up on the screen where he belongs, if I do say so myself!"

"That would be wonderful." The woman smiled up at Maria as she set a large latte down on the table and walked away. "I felt so bad for him during that time, you know, when his father died. And then his mother, when she couldn't go on."

Jen's head came up.

Cody was silent for a moment, then he said quietly, "Sure, and you've got a good heart to be worried about the lad. He had his troubles for a while, but I think he's gotten beyond them. At least, that's what it said in the paper I read."

"You think so? I just *love* his movies. I've seen every single one. And the way he rescued those two in that store—I just want things to go better for him."

Cody studied the woman for a long moment. "I believe you do. And bless you for that." He glanced in Maria's direction. "I can't stay here talking with you all afternoon, much as I'd like to. My boss is a fearsome woman with a terrible temper. She'll have me quaking in my boots if I don't continue to get things done around here."

As if in answer, Maria slammed some silverware around, and Cody jumped.

"You see what I mean? The woman's a terror. Now, is everything to your satisfaction?"

"Yes—except that I wish I'd really seen Cody."

"Keep your eyes open," Cody said. "Come to the big party we'll be throwing here tonight and enjoy the band." He smiled down at the woman, and Jen caught her breath at his charm. Cody glanced at her and winked, then directed his attention back to the woman.

"I'll keep my eye out for you tonight. It's close to Halloween, and the veil between the living and the dead is very thin. The most magical things can happen in this town on such a night."

LATE IN THE AFTERNOON CODY and Jen returned to Maria's house. All the lights had been hung, several pumpkins had been carved and set in strategic places and everything was as ready as it would ever be.

"Where did you get that Irish accent?" She had to know.

"Something I picked up while I was filming in Dublin."

"You really had that woman going. Not in a bad way."

Cody sighed. "Sometimes…it's not that I don't appreciate the people who go and see my movies. I do. But sometimes I'm just not in the mood. Colin comes in very handy."

"You've used him before?"

"That I have," he said, slipping into the Irish accent. His blue eyes darkened as he looked down at her and wrapped his arms around her waist. "And could I be talking this girl into taking a shower with me and washing away all the dust and grime before we get into our fancy clothes? I'm quite good at scrubbing a lady's back."

"I'll bet you are, Colin." She started to laugh as he led her toward the bathroom.

IN THE WAY THAT MOST PARTIES have, everything began to come together rapidly. Cody and Bob picked up the pizzas, the caterers brought the rest of the food—not enough, as Maria had predicted—and the band set up on the small stage in the far corner of the coffeehouse.

And then, at precisely sunset, the party began.

CODY HAD LOVED HER COSTUME from the moment he'd seen it.

"You should go into the business if you can make

costumes like that!" he'd said admiringly when she'd come out of the bathroom completely dressed in her Gypsy garb.

"You think so?" She'd twirled around, letting the tiered skirt flare out above her boots.

"Yeah."

"You don't look so bad yourself."

He'd dressed in tight black pants, a flowing white shirt and a red silk sash for a belt and had a black scarf knotted over his head. A gold hoop graced one of his ears, along with a fake tattoo high on one cheek. He hadn't shaved, so he had that extremely attractive stubble thing going. The costume also had a leather belt, complete with fake dagger and sword.

"I didn't have time to grow a beard," he'd told her. "I couldn't have, because of filming. But the next time I go out as a pirate, I promise you a full beard. The total fantasy."

"This," Jen had said, "will do quite well."

A BIT OF A BUZZ WAS PACKED, people crammed in wall to wall, the party in full swing, the band rocking the house. Candles flickered in fat pumpkins, their orange faces smiling wickedly. The scents of candle wax and pizza and Thai food mingled with the spicy pumpkin scent of the cookies.

"Cody," Jen said, a mischievous urge taking over, "you told me you wanted me to read your palm."

"That I did," he said, keeping in character as a pirate, grabbing her around the waist and swinging her into one of the chairs in a far corner of the crowded coffeehouse. "That I did."

He pulled up a chair close to hers, then stuck out his hands. "Which one do you want to see?"

"Are you right- or left-handed?" she asked, giving him what she hoped was a Gypsy's sultry stare. She'd put on a lot more eye makeup than she usually wore, and the effect had been striking.

"I use both of these hands to my best advantage," he said, and the look he gave her reminded her of other places and other, more sensual, times.

"Don't try to distract me! Right or left?"

"Right."

"Hand me your palm." Jen wasn't entirely sure she could do this. She'd taken a crash course in palm reading with Maria's detailed books, but now that she had Cody's hand in front of her, she wondered how well she would actually do.

"Hmm," she said as she studied the lines in his palm and began to pick them out; life line, head line, heart line. "After I'm done, you'll have to cross my palm in silver."

"Speaking of loot, do you see any chests of gold in my future?" Cody said, and she laughed, then gave his hand a squeeze and looked at it more intently.

"A strong life line. You've enjoyed mostly good health and have a very strong will to live."

"Yes," he said, and she got the feeling that he was wondering how she was doing this.

"You have a mystic cross between your head and your heart line," she continued. "That's a psychic mark. I would guess that you make most of your life decisions based on intuition, on a gut hunch, rather than on carefully analyzing the facts. And sometimes you sense things before they even happen." She wondered how he would take that observation.

"That's the truth, my fine wench. There's no other way for a pirate to be! You have to think fast on the high seas!"

A couple nearby laughed appreciatively at Cody's improvised dialogue, enjoying the fact that he was staying in character.

"Your heart line is strong and deep. You have a good heart and you act from your heart, not your head."

"Shhh," Cody said, his lips close to her ear. "I can't have any other pirates that might be lurking about knowing that I even *have* a heart."

That made her laugh.

"Ah, you have a very large Mount of Venus."

"And what in the name of the seven seas does *that* mean?"

She leaned close to him, so her lips almost touched his ear, and whispered, "It means you're an extremely sensual man."

"With certain fine wenches, that might be the case." He smiled at her, and she glanced away and back down at his palm, her face heating up.

"And here, down by the wrist, I see you possess a very special line. A *Via Lascivia*."

"What?" Cody said, and the look on his face almost made her burst out laughing. "A *Via what*?"

"It connects the Venus and Luna mounts—it suggests an unbridled sensuality and passion and a preoccupation with sexual excitement." She glanced up at him and knew her amusement was plain in her expression. "You'd be the sort of pirate who has a girl in every port."

He narrowed his eyes at her, then linked hands with her and brought her hand up and kissed it.

"If my passion is unbounded, it's for only one girl and in only one port."

"I like that," she said, turning her face up for his kiss.

THE PARTY WAS A COMPLETE AND total success. Maria was over the moon at the good time everyone was having, and Jen couldn't remember the last time she'd had so much fun at a gathering the size of this one.

Cody had found the blond woman—Dolores—and was dancing with her on the small space they'd designated as a dance floor, by the band. Jen had watched, totally touched, as the woman had almost had a coronary when she'd realized that the actual Cody Roberts had asked her to dance with him. And they looked as if they were having a glorious time.

Maria came up behind her and put a hand on her shoulder. Someone jostled her, but she regained her balance as she put her lips next to Jen's ear.

"This is the best!" she said. The noise in the place was deafening, and Jen barely heard her. She nodded her head. Maria looked stunning in her *Moulin Rouge*-inspired costume.

Then her friend saw Cody with Dolores and started to laugh. She was still laughing as Bob caught her hand and pulled her out onto the makeshift dance floor.

Jen watched them all dance, then made her way

through the crowd until she was at one of the low counters. Hoisting herself up onto it, she sat there, totally happy and in the moment. At that exact instant she knew she'd made the right decision to come out to California and start her life over.

She didn't know if making cookies for Maria would evolve into her lifetime career. She did know that what she had with Cody was something incredibly special. But she also knew that none of it would have happened if she hadn't had the courage to pack up her car and hit the road in search of the woman she'd lost—herself.

She touched her wrist absently, missing the feel of the gold bracelet she'd worn the morning of the robbery. It reminded her of her father. Their relationship was not going well. Other than a few more terse phone calls, she hadn't spoken to him. He still didn't understand what she was doing. He didn't even know that she was seeing Cody, and she saw no sense in telling him and upsetting him even more. She'd wait, bide her time....

She was watching Cody dancing with Dolores when her cell phone rang. Reaching into the pocket of her Gypsy skirt, she flipped the phone open and glanced at the number in the display. Arizona area code.

For an instant she was puzzled. Cody was back from filming. Who would be calling her from Arizona? Then comprehension dawned as she remembered Johnny, the salesclerk from the convenience store, and his mother, Laura. They were such sweet people; no doubt they were calling to wish her a happy Halloween.

She turned and slipped over the counter, then walked in back, to one of the storerooms, and shut the door behind her. The noise immediately lessened, and she spoke into the cell.

"Hello?"

No answer.

"Hello? Laura? Johnny?"

She heard someone take a hesitant breath on the line.

"Johnny?" she said softly. Perhaps it was all just hitting the boy now, and he'd wanted to call her, someone who'd been there, someone who would understand. She had to make sure he felt safe talking to her.

"Johnny, is that you?" she said. "Talk to me."

"Jennifer?"

Laura, Johnny's mother. The woman with the kind eyes, the woman who had been so very gentle and understanding to her that awful morning almost a month ago. And her voice sounded so strange.

"Laura? What's wrong?"

"It's Johnny." The woman caught her breath, and Jen heard all the emotion behind this mother's words. "It's Johnny, and—he's not doing too good. Oh, Jen, I don't know how to say this, but—I need your help."

12

As soon as Cody found out that Jen had received the phone call from Laura, Jen had a true education in what being a star meant.

She'd always known that the idea of being a star meant that the public saw them as above the ordinary, with a life so extraordinary that the regular rules often didn't apply. But she'd never seen it brought home so succinctly, the differences between her and Cody, as it was within the hour after that phone call.

Cody grasped the emotional urgency of the situation immediately and made exactly one phone call—to a studio head who had been a major mentor to him while he'd been coming up. He'd asked for just one favor—use of his private jet.

Cody not only got the jet, the man he called made sure they had a car waiting once they touched down in Phoenix.

She'd never flown on a private jet before, and Jen knew she would've enjoyed the experience had the situation not been so urgent.

"He's not suicidal," she told Cody as the jet streaked through the night. The flight to Phoenix was a short one, but the jet saved them incredible time, not having to go through the hassle of getting tickets, waiting in lines, going through as elaborate a security check.

Instead they'd rushed back to Maria's house and changed into regular clothing instead of their costumes, and a sleek black car had come to the house and raced them to LAX in record time.

"He's starting to fail emotionally. He's starting to break down," Cody said with such assurance that Jen looked at him with new eyes.

"How did you know?"

"That work I did with trauma. During a difficult time in my life."

"What happened with that therapist Johnny was seeing?" Jen said, trying to put the puzzle together.

"My guess is that he didn't quite know what he was really dealing with. Or Johnny didn't tell him the truth."

Within the hour they'd touched down in Phoenix, gotten their car, and, Cody at the wheel and perfectly calm—at least, a lot calmer than Jen felt—they headed out toward Johnny's house.

LAURA ANSWERED THE DOOR. She'd been expecting them.

"He won't come out of his room," she whispered to Cody, and Jen saw how she instinctively turned toward this man's strength. "He can't seem to let go of what happened to him that morning."

"He never saw that therapist?" Cody said.

"A few visits. They didn't seem to do any good."

"Where's his father?" Cody said.

"He's not here. He's in Colorado. Burt drives a

truck and he's on the road a great deal of the time. He must be up somewhere in the mountains—I can't seem to get him on his cell phone. My daughter's at a sleepover. I knew Johnny wasn't doing well, but everything seemed to come to a head tonight." She took a deep breath. "I got scared. I didn't know who to call, and then I thought of Jen."

"I'm glad you called us," Jen said.

"Johnny always liked you. I thought—maybe you could help him."

"We can try," she said with much more confidence than she felt.

"Thank you both for coming so quickly," Laura said, and Jen, seeing the tears standing out in the woman's eyes, gave her hand a reassuring squeeze.

Cody turned toward Jen. "Do you think he'd have an easier time talking with you or me?"

"I'll try."

And with Cody and Laura right behind her, Jen started down the hall of the small stucco house.

"Johnny? It's me, Jen." She sat right outside his locked bedroom door. No light shone beneath the bottom of the door, and she knew the boy was sitting in the dark, alone.

Not a good place to be.

"Johnny?"

No answer.

It's not like I can say I was just in the neighborhood. She decided to get straight to the point.

"I'm worried about you," she said, keeping her voice calm and reassuring.

No answer.

"Are you in there?"

A short hesitation, then he said, "Yeah."

"Can you talk to me about it?"

"There's nothing to talk about," the boy answered.

"I don't think that's true. You helped me through a really difficult time, Johnny."

"Yeah, right."

"You did."

"I didn't do anything."

"You did," she said. "You protected me."

Another hesitation, then he spoke. "I was a big coward, Jen. It was all on that stupid tape, and they kept showing it on television at night, over and over again. How scared I was. I cried like a girl."

For a moment she didn't know what to say. Then she knew.

"Have people been…teasing you about it?"

"Well, yeah. Just about everyone at school."

She closed her eyes for a moment, knowing how painful that kind of cruel teasing could be. The thought of it angered her, and she knew that somehow she and Cody had to find the words to reach this boy.

"How can they know what we went through, Johnny? How can they possibly know?"

Silence.

Jen found herself so mad at those so-called friends of his, she wanted to spit.

"How does anyone know what they'd do until they're right in the middle of it?"

Silence again, then he said, "How are you doing?"

Good. He was thinking outside his own pain, and that was a good sign. But he was still denying his own.

"Sometimes not so good, Johnny. I used to have some pretty bad nightmares. But I've been getting better. And I've had some help."

"From a shrink?"

"No," she said, keeping her voice calm. *Keep him talking, keep him engaged, and we can get to the bottom of this. Keep him connected. Let him know we care.* "From Cody."

Big silence, then he exclaimed, "Cody Roberts? That guy? The big hero action star?"

Jen looked at Cody sitting right outside the closed door with her, Laura at his side.

"Cody," he said to Johnny. "Just Cody."

"You're here?" Johnny practically squeaked the words out.

"Jen and I were concerned about you," Cody said, then glanced at Laura. "We were in the area—I was doing some publicity—and we thought we'd just stop by. Your mom had told us if we were ever in the area just to stop by. I know it's a little late, but we both wanted to see you."

Thank you, mouthed Laura silently, her expression still anxious.

"Wow," Johnny said, then the words seemed to rush out in a torrent. "Cody, how did you know what to do? How come you weren't scared—"

"I was terrified."

"But you do that sort of stuff all the time. You're this big hero."

"I'm not a hero, Johnny. I'm just a man."

Silence while Johnny thought about this.

"It's different in a movie," Cody continued. "The whole thing's all scripted out, and if it really gets dangerous, the studio insists that I use a stuntman."

"You use a stuntman?"

Cody laughed, then said, "They wouldn't insure me if I didn't. His name's Danny Robards. He's a great guy. I tell you what—the next action movie I do, I'll have you on the set one of the days we shoot some of the stunts. It's not at all what it looks like when it ends up on the screen."

"Huh."

"It's scripted, Johnny, and it's rehearsed. You didn't have that luxury. You had some guy crash his way in the door before you even had a moment to think. But you thought of protecting Jen. You made sure you were between her and that shotgun. I don't know how well I would have done if I'd been in your place."

"I don't believe that."

"Believe it," Cody said. "Believe it, because I had a few minutes' heads-up when I saw that jerk start inside the store. I saw you behind the counter and Jen by the coffee and I decided to come up with a plan to get all of us out."

Jen met his eyes, then looked away. A bit of a white lie, but Johnny didn't need to know that. That morning, Cody hadn't really cared if he'd made it.

"The tape," Johnny said. "I keep seeing it over and over. Me crying like a girl, and you getting that guy."

"He was twice your size," Cody said. "And high on something. It was hard for me to bring him down."

"It was?"

Something in those two words told Jen that they were getting through to Johnny. She reached for Laura's hand and smiled at the woman, who was looking less edgy and more relaxed as Cody continued to talk to Johnny.

"Johnny, you caught me on a good day that morning," Cody said, his voice calm. Even.

A hesitation, then Johnny said, "I can't imagine a guy like you screwing up just about anything."

"Hey, you're comparing your insides to my outsides. Not a good idea, because my publicist makes it look like being a movie star is the best career on the planet."

"Huh."

Cody moved a little closer to the closed bedroom door. "You want to know when I felt a lot like you do now?" Cody said as casually as if he were asking about the weather.

"Yeah."

"When my dad died. It was a really senseless accident on the ranch. It was sudden, and none of us were prepared for it." Cody took a deep breath, then said, "I felt so powerless, like nothing I would ever do or say again would make any difference."

"Yeah," Johnny said, and the one word said it all. Jen knew what the boy was really saying. *I know that feeling. I'm there right now.*

"My mom died about eight weeks later. She couldn't go on without him."

"What did you do?" Johnny asked.

"I'm not real proud of what I did. I was working

as an actor, but I went on a real rampage. I drank myself blind, I screwed up some friendships, I pissed some people off so badly, it's a miracle we're still speaking. And I really messed up my career."

"You did? *You?*"

"Me. I let a lot of people down because I couldn't get past my own pain. I did a lot of stuff that wasn't too smart because I just wanted the pain to stop instead of working through it."

Jen, her head leaning against the hallway wall, watched Cody as he made contact with the boy. In the strangest of ways and at a very strange time, all the doubts she might have had about her relationship with Cody simply vanished. Disappeared.

If she'd ever felt she was out of Cody's league or didn't belong in his world, she didn't anymore. She'd given him the gift of seeing himself for who he was, for loving the man that he was, not the heroic, larger-than-life image he projected as part of his work.

He'd been a real hero to her and for her, a man frightened to death in a horrific situation, but one who had had the courage to act despite his fear. Yet underneath he was just a man, and Jen had a feeling that not too many people in his life let him just be a man.

He would never have to be some sort of projection or fantasy with her. Just Cody.

"I want the pain to stop, too," Johnny said, his words barely audible.

"I'll help you get there, Johnny, I promise," Cody said, and Jen felt the reassurance in his voice.

Another silence as Johnny digested what Cody had told him. Then he said, "Really? You messed up?"

"What?" Cody said, teasing. "You don't read the tabloids? How badly I screwed up? Man, they had me on the front page for *months.*"

"My mom doesn't let us read that stuff."

"Smart woman."

"How did you—" Johnny said hesitantly. "How did you get things back? The way they were?"

That question tore at Jen's heart, and her eyes filled. She remembered looking at her grandmother and asking her, *When is Mommy coming back? Why does she want to be up in heaven and not down here with me?*

"They can never go back to the way they were," Cody said, his words as sharp and sure as a surgeon's blade, though his tone was gentle. "I tried to keep the ranch exactly as it was, but without my parents there it wasn't the same. I finally realized that and sold it and bought another piece of property north of Santa Barbara and took some of our horses with me."

Jen thought about his life as she listened, wondering what it could be like to lose your entire family within the space of a couple of months. Cody had truly been through emotional hell.

Cody continued speaking to the boy, his voice low and intent. "Johnny, you have to go back to your life, no matter what those assholes at school are saying. No matter what's happened, you just have to go on. It's your life and you have to live it as best you can. And they don't know anything, those kids at school. They must be hurting real bad themselves if they have to torment you."

Silence.

"But how do you get past it?" the boy finally said. "I don't think—I don't know if I can."

"Can I come in there and ask you a few questions?" Cody said, and Jen knew he was referring to the questions he'd asked her in the motel room in the middle of the night. The questions he'd learned as a part of his work with traumatized people.

"Like a shrink?"

"No. Like a friend. We could just talk. Man to man."

Jen held her breath, then watched in wonder as the bedroom door slowly opened and Johnny peered out. He'd lost weight and his eyes had that scared expression she'd seen in her own when she'd looked in the mirror.

He stared at Cody, and Jen suddenly realized that Cody hadn't had time to thoroughly wash his face and still sported that pirate tattoo on his cheek.

"It really is you," Johnny said as he stared at Cody. Then he smiled. "That's a cool tattoo."

"Aw, don't go all Hollywood on me," Cody said, then grinned.

JEN WENT BACK INTO THE KITCHEN with Laura. The woman made a pot of coffee, then got out a pound cake she'd baked earlier in the day. She cut a few slices, and they sat down and waited.

"I can't thank both of you enough for coming tonight," she said.

"It's okay," Jen said, setting down her coffee cup. "You were so great to me that day in the store, when the police were there."

"You both looked so frightened." Laura's eyes

filled again. "I took one look at both of you and wished it had been me instead."

Jen shook her head. "The longer I live, the more I think things happen for a reason." She glanced in the direction of Johnny's room. "Don't worry, Laura. He's in good hands with Cody."

"That man," Laura said as she picked up her mug, "is extraordinary."

"HE'S SLEEPING," CODY SAID AS he walked into the kitchen.

"Coffee?" Laura asked.

"Please."

"Did you ask him the same set of questions you asked me?" Jen said.

"Yeah."

"Where did you learn them?"

Cody took a sip of his coffee, then reached for a piece of cake. "When the worst of my rampage was over, I couldn't see going back to acting. I stayed out at the ranch and tried to run it. And I heard about some people from the Red Cross who'd helped a neighboring town when a tornado hit, and they'd talked about how they helped people who had experienced severe trauma. At the time I thought acting was a useless thing to do, so I decided to do something like that."

"You worked for the Red Cross? I didn't see that in any of the tabloids."

"How many papers do you think that little bit of information would sell?" Cody said. "They usually want the sensational stuff."

"What happened? How did you go back to acting?"

Cody leaned back in his kitchen chair. "Have either of you ever seen a movie called *Sullivan's Travels?*"

Jen shook her head, and Laura did the same.

"It's about this guy who makes comedies and thinks what he does is useless, so he decides to travel the country and do something worthwhile. By this quirk of fate, he gets thrown in jail and learns what a hard life is really like. And at one of the breaks in their endless workdays, he sees the inmates watching a cartoon and laughing. It's the one great moment of their entire day. And he gets it."

"Gets what?" Laura said, fascinated.

"Gets that entertaining people, giving them something to laugh about or get caught up in or something to care about when their life is difficult, giving them a break from the sadness and the craziness of it all, well, I think it's a pretty good thing to do."

"So do I," whispered Jen, and Cody turned in his chair and smiled at her. *Heroic, in fact.* And she realized here was another thing she loved about Cody. He never really gave up. It might have looked like it when he'd been headed into the downward spiral so lovingly described by the tabloid press.

But Cody, in her opinion, was a true hero. He cared about people and he would keep doing whatever needed to be done, no matter how scared or tired or frustrated with life he was.

He was one of the good guys—and he was hers.

THEY LEFT LAURA VERY LATE that same night and told her they would come by in the morning.

"The worst should be over," Cody told her as Jen stood by his side on the front porch of the small house. "Those questions are designed to debrief a person when they've been in the midst of severe trauma. You feel the feelings, you're able to process them and then they don't rush up inside you and take over or cause you to shut down and get depressed."

"I'd like you both to come for lunch tomorrow. Please?"

Jen could tell that the woman wanted to thank them for coming to her aid.

"We'd love to," she said.

BACK IN THE CAR, JEN ASKED Cody, "You don't mind stopping by tomorrow, do you?"

"No, not at all. It'd be a good idea just to check on Johnny and see how he's doing."

"We should find a place," she said, then yawned.

"I have a plan," Cody said, and she glanced at him.

"Should I be worried?"

"Nah. This one's easy."

When he pulled into the parking lot of the motel just a few miles down from the convenience store and Johnny's home, Jen had to laugh.

"Oh, no, it'll be all over the news! Cody Roberts returns to the scene of the crime!"

"Darlin'," he said, giving her a quick kiss, "I think Colin's going to sweet-talk his way into a room tonight. They'll never know Cody was even here."

HE GOT THEM THE EXACT SAME room. Number seventeen.

"The only problem," Cody said, "is that the bathroom's too damn small for the two of us to take a shower together."

"A small price to pay for the sentimental value," Jen said, kicking off her shoes.

"Sleepy?" he said.

"I'm so sleepy that if I don't sleep soon, I'm going to be sick." She stripped off her clothing as she talked, flinging it on a nearby chair.

"Good plan," he said, removing his own clothing and sliding into bed beside her.

A CHILD YELLING IN THE PARKING lot woke Jen up. Early-morning sunlight filtered in beneath the curtains, and she stretched, then rolled over in the queen-size bed to see Cody awake, waiting.

"Hey," she said, then leaned over and kissed him.

"A good way to start the day," he said as they broke apart.

"I can think of something even better," she said, teasing him.

"I can think of something even better than that," he said, and she frowned, lying back on the pillow and looking up at him.

"Better? Really?"

"Yeah."

Something in his eyes changed—the color seemed to get richer and stronger. She could lose herself in those eyes; she could wake up to them every single day of her life. And suddenly she knew what he was going to do, what was even better than starting the day with lovemaking.

"Cody," she breathed, barely hoping. "Oh, Cody."

"Yeah," he said, and she saw him slide his hand out from beneath his pillow, a small black velvet ring box in that same hand.

"Oh my God," she whispered. "Oh my God." Only a month. Too soon, too soon...

"I love you, Jen," he said, and she saw the emotion in his eyes, pure and strong. "I want to spend the rest of my life with you and I want that life to get started as soon as possible."

She couldn't look away from those eyes. And suddenly none of it mattered—the short time they'd known each other, the strange way their paths had intersected. Nothing mattered but the man in front of her and the expression in his eyes.

"Cody," she breathed, words failing her.

"I know it's barely been a month, but I knew right away that you were special. You were right. For me. We can have as long an engagement as you want, but I don't want you to have any doubts as to how I feel about you."

"Were you going to ask me—"

"I was going to ask you after the party, but then Laura called. I'm glad we were able to help Johnny, but I also wanted to ask you, and it seemed...right. It seemed right to do it here."

She'd started to cry, wiping at the tears that were running down her face.

He pulled her close against him. So close, their bodies were touching. "Jen, will you marry me?"

"Yes," she said. "Yes."

He slid the ring on her finger and then kissed her, and then they made love. And it was different, knowing they were going to spend the rest of their lives together, helping each other, loving each other, facing the world and everything it might bring together.

And afterward, before sleep claimed her, she reached for his hand and squeezed it tightly.

"Cody?"

"Hmm." He sounded happily satiated.

"Thank you for being my hero. Thank you for rescuing me."

He kissed her shoulder. They were curled up like spoons, bodies touching, their heads on the same pillow, as close as two people could be.

"And I don't just mean that morning at the convenience store," she whispered.

"I know, Jen."

She thought he was going to remain silent, but he put his arm around her, warm, hard-muscled and strong, and whispered against her ear, "It works both ways."

"You think so?" she said sleepily.

"I know so. You rescued me right back."

"Okay," she said, and he laughed.

"Get some sleep," he whispered. "I've set the clock so we'll have time to get ready for Laura's lunch."

"Uh-huh," she whispered back, and he laughed softly, knowing she was already partially asleep.

"I'll be here when you wake up, Jen," he said, liking the sound of the words, the promise contained in them, even though he knew she was no longer listening. "And every day after that. Forever."

He moved closer, his face against the softness of

her hair, and closed his eyes, breathing in that unique scent that was hers alone.

And Cody thought with a quiet sort of amazement that life was very good. He'd run just about as far as a man could run and fallen about as far as a man could fall.

But now, with Jen in his arms and knowing he had a future with her, Cody Roberts found that he was finally, finally at peace.

1

DALLAS SHEA CHECKED her watch and then shoved her keys and two twenties into her jeans pocket. She'd planned on walking the eighteen blocks up to midtown, but now she had to catch a cab or she'd be late.

"Oh, good, you're still here." Her roommate burst out of the tiny bathroom they shared while she pulled her long red hair up into a ponytail. Behind her, a heap of towels lay near the foot of the ancient claw tub.

Dallas sighed. The woman was the consummate slob. Funny, spontaneous, ambitious and a loyal friend, but a total slob. "Not for long. I'm on my way out."

"Can you walk Bruiser first?"

"No."

The furry black mutt heard his name and came from behind the green floral couch, which was the extent of their tiny living room, wagging his tail, looking up at Dallas with soulful black eyes. He had to be up to seven pounds by now—big difference from three months ago when Wendy had found him scrounging for food in an alley near Nineteenth Street.

"Please, Dallas. I'll make dinner."

Giving Wendy a dry look, Dallas headed for the

door, trying to avoid looking at Bruiser. If she did, she'd give in. "That's what you said the last time."

"I came through, didn't I?"

"Hot dogs from Howie's cart is not my idea of dinner."

"Come on, please. I have an audition." Wendy hopped on one leg as she pulled on a tennis shoe over her purple tights. "It's really important. A new Neil Simon musical and they need twelve dancers. This time I'm going to get it. I know it. Right here." She pressed a palm to her tummy. "This is gonna be my big break."

Dallas undid the dead bolt. Then she hesitated, all the while reminding herself this wasn't her business. But Wendy was crazy for chasing after these jobs. Sadly, at twenty-nine, she was already too old for Broadway. A new crop of eager, energetic young twentysomethings were getting all the gigs.

She looked at her friend, and then down at Bruiser, whose expectant eyes met hers, his tail still wagging. Even he had already figured out what a pushover Dallas was.

Sighing, she opened the door for Wendy. "Go."

Grinning, Wendy hopped toward her as she slid on her other sneaker. "You're the best."

"Be careful of those feet. I need your share of the rent." Dallas scooped up Bruiser before he made a break for the open door, and then grabbed his leash off the hook on the wall. "Don't worry about dinner. I'm meeting Trudie."

"Tell her I said hey."

"Break a leg," Dallas said as Wendy slipped out into the hall and closed the door.

She put Bruiser down and crouched to secure his leash. "What are you looking at me like that for? Huh?" She stroked his curly black fur, laughed when he licked her chin, rearing back just in the nick of time to avoid a sloppy kiss.

"Okay, boy, I know it's been a while since I've had a date, but I like my guys a little taller." She stood, grabbing the plastic bag she needed to clean up after Bruiser.

In a way she envied Wendy. She never gave up. Her optimism and enthusiasm seemed boundless. Even after she'd lost the contract with Revalyn last year. A week after her twenty-eighth birthday, the company had decided they needed someone with younger-looking hands for their print ads. Thank God feet didn't age as quickly.

Dallas sighed. Boy, was she glad she'd gotten out of that world quickly. She'd modeled for a year during her senior year in college. After the blowup with her parents and she'd been cut off, she'd needed the money. But that was enough. There had always been someone taller, slimmer, prettier. She'd hated every minute of it.

She led Bruiser out of the apartment, careful to double lock the door, then checked her watch as she waited for the elevator, hoping the damn thing wasn't on a milk run. Of course, that it was working at all was cause for celebration. If she had the money she'd move out, but finding and affording another apartment without having to move to Brooklyn would mean working a whole lot of overtime. Or worse, taking another job. The kind her parents would approve of. The thought made her shudder.

"THANK GOD YOU'RE HERE." Trudie looked up from a pink phone slip on her desk, her heavily outlined brown eyes filled with worry. "Close the door, would you?"

"Sure." Dallas did as asked and then dropped into the worn burgundy leather guest chair. "What's up?"

"I'm totally screwed."

Dallas tried not to smile. Her friend had a penchant for drama. Their circle of college friends had been certain Trudie would end up on Broadway, not dressing department-store windows. "What's wrong?"

"I'm in charge of doing the Fifth Avenue window display for the Fourth of July sale. It's also the store's tenth anniversary."

"Sounds like a big deal."

"Yes," Trudie said miserably. "And I'm about to blow it big-time."

"How?"

Trudie shoved the pink slip she'd been studying across her crowded desk, between a stack of fashion magazines and a pile of fabric swatches.

Dallas picked up the phone message. It was from someone named Starla Jenkins. It simply said she had a stomach virus and had to cancel tomorrow evening.

"Okay," Dallas said slowly, sliding the pink slip back toward Trudie. Her friend was obviously upset, so she decided to forgo the wisecrack that came to mind. "And?"

"I am so screwed."

"Who's Starla Jenkins?"

"A model I'd hired." Trudie exhaled sharply. "Stomach virus, my ass. I haven't heard of anything going around."

"So? I'm sure there are fifteen others who'd love to take her place. Call the agency."

"It's not that simple," Trudie said, and then remained silent as she stared at Dallas with an odd expression on her face. Her gaze dropped to Dallas's hands and she wrinkled her nose. "Your nails are horrible."

Dallas reflexively balled them into fists. "I just got off work."

"That's okay." Trudie flashed her a quick smile. "We can fix them."

"I don't want them fixed." She studied her friend for a moment, a bad feeling growing in the pit of her stomach. "Look, if you need to cancel dinner so you can find a replacement, I totally understand."

Trudie's gaze stayed steady. "I already have."

Dallas stared back, feeling uneasy. Trudie couldn't possibly be thinking— No, of course not. Ridiculous. She knew better. But just in case… "No."

"Come on, Dallas. I'm not asking you to do it for nothing."

"Why ask me, period? You could find a replacement in half an hour."

"No way, Toots." Trudie shook her head. "I promised my manager something special. A live mannequin."

Dallas's mouth opened but didn't cooperate any further.

"*You* gave me the idea," Trudie said in an accusatory tone. "Remember how in college you used to fake everyone out? Jill and I would take bets you could stay perfectly still for a half hour at a time. Hell, we used to clean up. Pay for all our gas and entertainment."

"That was eight years ago."

"You did it again at the Christmas party last year and took fifty bucks off that snobby Chandler Whitestone."

"That was different. He ticked me off."

"Please, Dallas. You have to bail me out."

Dallas sighed. Did she have *sucker* written across her forehead or something? "I have faith you'll find someone else. Or come up with another window display."

"By tomorrow?"

"I'm not standing in a damn department-store window. I'm too out of shape."

"Bull. You should never have left the business." Trudie glanced at Dallas's hands again. "Your nails suck, but other than that you're every bit as pretty and—"

"I'm twenty-nine."

Trudie's mouth twisted wryly. "There's that."

Dallas stood. "Moot point. Are we doing dinner or not?"

"Look, my career's on the line here." Trudie hesitated. "I wouldn't ask if I wasn't desperate."

"Have you *even tried* to find someone else?"

"Yes. I swear."

Dallas sank back into the chair. She believed her. Trudie wasn't one to ask for favors. Even after her shithead of a boyfriend had moved out along with half of Trudie's furniture and the next month's rent, she hadn't asked Dallas or Wendy for a thing. Hadn't accepted anything that was offered, either.

"Come on, Dallas. As soon as Starla gets over her virus or whatever, she'll call and you'll be off the hook."

"I'm not on the hook."

"Oh, God, are you going to make me beg? Do I have to get down on my knees?"

Dallas sighed, knowing she was going to regret this. "Okay," she said slowly. "How long do I have to pose, and what do I have to wear?"

Trudie's smile faltered. "Come on, let's go have a drink or two first."

"Trudie…"

Her friend got up from her desk, grabbed her purse and headed out the door. "I'm buying."

Dallas followed. She was not going to like this. Not one bit.

ERIC HARMON PAID the cab driver and got out near Sixth and Lexington. No sign of Tom. He checked his watch. Traffic had been surprisingly cooperative, and he'd apparently beaten his friend to the rendezvous point a block from their office where they both worked for Webber and Horn Advertising.

He squinted up at the twentieth floor and counted four windows from the corner, which was Tom's office. The light was still on. But of course so was the light in Eric's office, two over from Tom's, and Eric had no intention of returning to work. Not today. He was too beat.

They really should've met at Pete's Grille, he realized. After the meeting he had just left, he could really use a double Scotch about now. He checked his watch again, moved out of the way as a horde of pedestrians left the crosswalk and headed for him, and then withdrew his cell phone from his suit jacket pocket.

"Put that away. I'm right behind you."

He turned toward Tom's voice and slid the phone back into his pocket. "I need a drink."

"Me, too."

Eric looked down at the briefcase his friend was holding. "Since when do you take work home?"

Tom shook his head, his expression grim. "I don't care how badly your meeting went, be damn glad you weren't in the office this afternoon."

"Great. Tell me it doesn't have to do with the Mercer account." The advertising business could be a bitch. When you bonded with the client, you were on top of the world. But then there were those times you thought about ordering a one-way ticket to Siberia.

"I'm not talking work until after I have a Scotch." Tom stepped back, accidentally bumping into a short blonde in a khaki suit. "Excuse me."

At his dimpled smile, her irritation promptly vanished. "No problem." She returned the smile, laced with a brief but obvious invitation.

Eric sighed. "Come on, Romeo. Let's get to Pete's before your wife calls and tells you to get your ass home."

Tom gave the blonde's swaying rear end a final appreciative look before turning toward Fourth Avenue. "Speaking of wives, since *you* don't have one," Tom said as if it were a crime, "who are you taking to Webber's annual thanks-for-the-job-well-done-but-you're-not-getting-a-bonus party?"

"Who says I have to take anyone?"

"Unspoken rule, my friend. You always show up and you don't show up alone. The guy's old-school. He thinks everyone should be married and settled by the time they're thirty. A mark you've already passed. Besides, didn't you get the picture after the Christmas party? He didn't like it that you were the only one flying solo."

Eric scoffed. "That attitude's not only ridiculously antiquated, it's illegal."

"Tell him that." Tom's head swung around after a redheaded jogger in a skintight green tank and running shorts who'd passed them.

"And then there are some guys who just shouldn't be married."

"What?" Tom glanced at him and laughed. "Only looking, pal. Only looking. Something you should be doing more of before everyone starts thinking you're light on the feet."

Eric snorted, tempted to remark on the blond highlights Tom had streaked through his light brown hair every month. Talk about looking as if he batted for the other team.

Frankly he didn't know how Tom did it. Juggle a wife, a successful but demanding career and an active and strategic social life. Of course, Tom's first putt in life came with a handicap. Prominent Westchester family. Ivy League education. No student loans to repay. A wife with an impressive social pedigree.

Must be nice. Eric wouldn't know. His background was Pittsburgh blue collar all the way. Of his entire extended family he'd been the first to graduate from college and escape a life sweating in the steel mills.

"Seriously, Eric," he continued, "when was the last time you brought someone to a company function?"

"Why are we discussing this?"

"Tell me when and I'll drop it."

"Why would I subject a date to one of Webber's boring parties?" He was about to cross the street when the light turned red. Normally that wouldn't stop him, except a stretch limo came barreling around the corner from Lexington.

"See? Good reason to get married. Then the girls gotta go and be bored."

"Right."

Tom elbowed him. "Check out the blonde at three o'clock. The one in the red stiletto heels."

Eric casually glanced in that direction. "Not bad."

"Not bad? Are you nuts? That one could put you in intensive care for a month."

Eric started to cross the street as soon as the light changed. Two cabs ran the red light and honked at the pedestrians who'd entered the crosswalk. Across the street several other cabs blasted their horns for no apparent reason. You'd never know the city imposed a $350-dollar fine for unnecessary honking.

They'd barely made it across Fifth Avenue when Tom started in again. "Okay, I want you to point out your idea of the perfect woman." He gestured toward the mass of people, mostly women in suits and running shoes, coming toward them. "You have a wide variety right here."

"What is with you today?"

"Humor me."

Eric shook his head in disgust, at the same time catching sight of a department-store window display, taken aback by the realistic beach scene. Sand, sun, a threatening wave that looked as if it were about to crash over two incredibly lifelike mannequins and then right through the window onto the sidewalk. Computer generated, obviously, but realistic enough to earn some gasps from the crowd of onlookers and send an older couple back several steps.

Remarkable as the special effects were, what caught his attention was the blond mannequin in the red bikini. She looked so damn real. And perfect. Long honey-blond hair, sexy blue eyes, full lips that formed a tempting bow. And man, did she have legs....

"Are you listening?" Tom got in his face.

"What?" Eric hadn't realized he'd stopped. Right in the middle of the sidewalk, blocking everyone's way. People muttered curses and stepped around him. "No."

He looked back at the window. At the mannequin. She was amazing. Incredible. Too bad that kind of perfection could only be synthetic.

Tom followed his gaze just as another wave swelled threateningly, and he ducked. Clearly realizing his foolish reaction, he straightened and glanced around. Several other onlookers had done the same.

"Damn, that's amazing."

Eric nodded. "Genius. Pure genius. Look at how many people the window's attracting."

"No shit. This should earn someone a nice little bonus."

Eric shook his head. Lately, with Tom, it was always about money or women. As if he needed to worry about either. "Let's go."

"Wait. No more changing the subject. You have an assortment of lovelies right here. Blondes, brunettes, redheads." Ignoring a sharp look he received from a well-dressed older woman who'd obviously overheard, he gestured toward a group staring at the window. "I'm not moving until you choose one."

Eric shrugged and turned to leave. "I'll say hey to everyone at Pete's for you."

Tom snagged his coat sleeve. "Come on."

Eric sighed. His gaze went back to the mannequin, to the tiny beauty mark at the corner of her lush mouth. "Her," he said with a jut of his chin.

"Who?" Tom scanned the group of women close to the window. "Which one?"

"There." Eric barely contained a smile as he fixed his gaze on the mannequin. "She's perfect."

It took Tom a moment for it to register, and then he laughed. "Why, because she can't talk?"

"A big bonus, you have to admit."

"I'll give you that." Tom studied the mannequin. "Great legs, too. I wonder if she's busy this weekend."

Eric shook his head, and headed across the street. "I'm gonna go have a drink. You do what you want."

Tom had started after him when he heard the crowd gasp. He turned just in time to see the two mannequins throwing their hands up as if frightened by the wave, and then they repositioned themselves, again going perfectly still.

The crowd began murmuring and talking excitedly, loud enough that Eric turned around to see what was happening. Tom took off after him.

"What's going on?" Eric asked.

"Nothing. Another wave." Tom shouldered him, urging him to keep walking. "Let's go before my keeper calls."

Tom could barely contain himself. This was rich. Totally awesome. He wasn't sure what he was going to do yet, but the opportunity for something really big was there.

Like Saturday night—the company dinner. God, this was too perfect.

In his excitement, he nearly tripped over his own feet.

All he had to do was keep Eric away from that window for the next two days.

SPOTLIGHT

A NEW 12-book series featuring the reader-favorite Fortune family launches in June 2005!

THE F RTUNES OF TEXAS: *Reunion*

Cowboy at Midnight

by *USA TODAY* bestselling author

ANN MAJOR

Rancher Steven Fortune considered himself lucky. He had a successful ranch, good looks and many female companions. But when the contented bachelor meets events planner Amy Burke-Sinclair, he finds himself bitten by the love bug!

The Fortunes of Texas: Reunion—
The power of family.

Exclusive Extras!
Family Tree...
Character Profiles...
Sneak Peek

Where love comes alive™

If you enjoyed what you just read,
then we've got an offer you can't resist!

Take 2 bestselling
love stories FREE!

Plus get a FREE surprise gift!

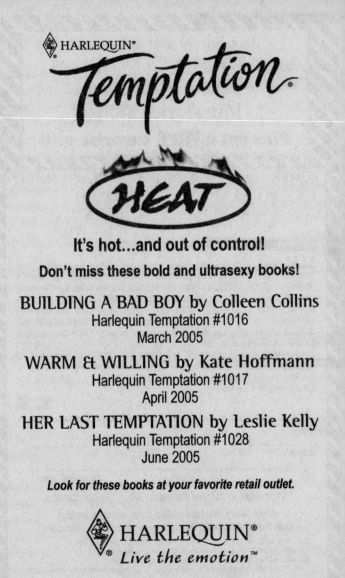